T̶ Chimera Jar

JAMES E. WISHER

James E. Wisher

The Aegis of Merlin:

The Impossible Wizard

The Awakening

The Chimera Jar

The Raven's Shadow

Edited by: Janie Linn Dullard

Cover Art by: Paganus

Sand Hill Publishing 423171.0

ISBN 13: 978-1-945763-11-3

Chapter 1

Teamwork

Conryu walked down the familiar hall to dark magic class with a mixture of relief and disappointment. Winter break had been a pleasant change of pace after months of magic studies, but he hadn't been able to avoid magic all together. The business with the Department remained fresh in his mind. Hopefully Mr. Kane would have the situation straightened out soon, if for no other reason than Maria was worried about him.

Prime wriggled in his grip. The scholomantic didn't like being carried and kept fidgeting in his hand. Right now Prime looked like nothing but an ugly green book. Conryu hid him between his notepad and *Infernal Basics* book.

So far he'd been able to keep Prime a secret from the other students, though he had no idea who Dean Blane had told. Only Mrs. Umbra had asked to see the scholomantic and that had been a brief inspection conducted ten minutes after he got back to school. She seemed neither impressed with Prime nor disappointed in Conryu for claiming him. That was about as good a reaction as he dared expect.

1

Prime had strict instructions to remain silent except when they were in his room and even then Conryu wasn't allowed to study any of the many secrets the book held, except as applied to whatever his teachers had him working on.

In addition to checking out Prime, Mrs. Umbra had said that they'd turned the investigation into the Grand Brawl incident over to the Department in Central. The only clue they'd found was a small fragment of necroplasma that had been made as hard as steel. It seemed the viper golem had been made of the stuff, but most of it dissolved when the demon escaped. He shuddered to think how many lives it took to create that much of the crud.

"Conryu!" Kelsie jogged down the hall to catch up to him.

He slowed and she fell in step beside him. When he hadn't run into her on the train or in their dorm Conryu feared she may have decided she didn't want to be friends after all. Her bright smile as she walked beside him argued otherwise.

"How was your winter break?" he asked.

"I survived. You?"

"It was interesting." No reason to give her too many details, especially since he had no idea what he could and couldn't talk about. "I did some fieldwork with Maria's mom, you know, to get a taste of the business of magic. Can't say I'm much more interested in it now than I was."

"I don't blame you. It seems like all my family talks about is business. I feel more like my mom's employee than her daughter sometimes."

"That's harsh." Conryu opened the classroom door for her.

The others turned to look when they entered. No one said anything, they just stared. It couldn't be just him. They had to be used to having a guy in the class by now. Maybe it was because he was hobnobbing with the rich and famous.

He shook his head and took his seat at the back of the class. When Kelsie sat beside him instead of in her usual spot up front Conryu raised an eyebrow.

"What? I can't sit beside my friend?"

"Sure you can. I was just surprised."

The door burst open and Mrs. Lenore hustled through. "Sorry, I got mixed up in something. Welcome back, everyone."

She set to drawing on the chalkboard. When she finished there was a group of stick figures around a spell circle. "So for the second half of the year we'll be focusing on group castings. Group castings allow individual wizards to combine their power to create more potent effects than they'd otherwise be able to. With each person added to the casting it grows more complex so we'll be limiting our groups to five."

Mrs. Lenore wrote out two words in Infernal, break and shatter. "We'll start working in pairs to create a combined breaking."

From behind her desk she took out metallic spheres covered in runes. "These will be your practice targets. One member of the group will chant 'break' to destroy the wards while the other chants 'shatter' to smash the orb. The spells protecting them are much more potent than those used in the wooden blocks we trained with earlier. Everyone pair up."

Before Conryu had a chance to look Kelsie's way Mrs. Lenore continued. "Conryu, you'll be working with me. For safety reasons you understand."

Conryu sighed, nodded, and walked down to the front of the class to join her. While the girls were talking and sorting themselves out Mrs. Lenore leaned close so no one could overhear. "It won't do any good to pair you up with one of the girls until you can modulate your power enough to match a weaker partner. As it stands now your power would do all the work and she'd get nothing out of the experience."

"So what am I really going to do?"

"I'll explain once the girls have started."

The groups were soon set and Mrs. Lenore watched them for a few minutes to make sure they were doing everything correctly. When she was satisfied she rejoined Conryu in the front of the room.

"So you were saying?"

"Right, modulation. You need to hold back enough of your power so you don't overwhelm your partners."

"That sounds kind of pointless. If the idea is to combine our powers to create a more potent effect why would I use less than my full power? I mean to match Kelsie I'd have to use like ten percent of my full strength and the combined casting would amount to less than a quarter of what I could do on my own. How is that beneficial?"

Her mouth opened and closed but no words came out. She looked a bit like a fish caught on the beach. After a moment she pulled herself together. "When you put it that way it makes no sense at all. Combined casting is what I always teach during second semester. It never even occurred to me that it wouldn't work for you."

She slumped and fell silent. He glanced back at the girls, but they were all engrossed in their practice. He put a hand on her shoulder and Mrs. Lenore looked up.

"What are we going to do? If the final is all about combined casting I guess I need to learn it."

She shook her head. "That's not really what it's about. It's just the breaking is of an order of magnitude stronger than what a single dark wizard can handle."

Conryu raised an eyebrow at that.

"Okay, an ordinary dark wizard. Sometimes I don't even know why you're in my class. If you took the final today you'd pass it with ease."

"For the sake of argument and the fact that we don't have enough people for only two groups, how could I work with weaker partners? We've established that lowering my own strength is useless. What could a second and third person do to make me stronger?"

She sat on the edge of her desk and rubbed her temples. "I'm not sure. A standard circle casting wouldn't work. It's designed to unite wizards of similar strength. The problem is fusing the energy flows into a coherent whole."

"When I helped Mrs. Umbra banish the demon serpent she drew out my power and directed it with a spell of her own. Would something like that work?"

"If you had the Death Stick and fifty years of experience, sure." Mrs. Lenore closed her eyes and sighed. "I don't know what to do. I'm a horrible teacher."

"Don't say that. This is new for everyone. I have class with Mrs. Umbra later. Would you mind if I mentioned the problem to her? She might have a suggestion."

"By all means. God knows you need someone other than me to help you."

* * *

Class ended and everyone but Conryu left for their free period. The moment the last girl closed the door behind her Prime shook the notepad off and flew in front of him.

"That woman is incompetent. I should be overseeing your instruction. Imagine, telling the most powerful wizard in the world that what he really needs to know is how to make himself weaker. Of all the stupid ideas I've heard over the millennia that one's right up there with 'Let's call Lord Beelzebub *Bug Eyes.*'"

"Don't be so critical. Mrs. Lenore's a good person. I'm afraid she's just a little out of her depth."

"I didn't say she wasn't a good human, I said she's an idiot. If she'd given it even a moment of thought she'd have realized her idea didn't even bear contemplation."

The ominous tapping of Mrs. Umbra's Death Stick sent Prime flying back to hide under his notepad. The head of dark magic was the only person Prime seemed to fear, not that Conryu blamed the scholomantic. She certainly had an intimidating presence. Despite that, Conryu found he was eager to see her again.

The door opened and the short, wrinkled figure in black hobbled in.

"Afternoon, Mrs. Umbra."

"Conryu. I trust that ill-mannered book has been behaving itself."

"Prime's been on his best behavior. I haven't told anyone about him yet. Is that the plan or can I let others know?"

"Up to you, but until you learn to cast spells through it, the scholomantic will be a point of vulnerability."

"Is that what you're going to teach me?" He sat up straighter. Anything that eliminated a potential weakness was of interest to him. "Before I forget, I have a question."

She hobbled down and sat behind the desk. "Oh?"

He briefly explained what had happened in his first class. "Anyway, it sounds like combination casting won't be of much use for me. I need to figure out some way to work with my classmates, if only for the final."

She nodded and tapped her chin. "Hey, book."

Prime flew up off the desk, but didn't speak.

"Do you have anything on fusion magic?"

Conryu had never heard of such a thing, but Prime flipped his pages before finally stopping. On the open page was an image of three wizards standing in a triangle formation. The two in the back rested their hands on the one in front's shoulders and the text described how to merge the three powers into one. It looked like exactly what he needed.

"Can I show this to Mrs. Lenore? She seemed really upset that she didn't know what to teach me."

"Let me see."

Prime flew over to allow Mrs. Umbra to read the pages. After a minute she nodded. "Very complete. That should solve your group casting problem. You have my permission to study those pages in your spare time, though don't experiment without one of your teachers present."

"Never crossed my mind."

Prime flew back and landed on the desk.

Conryu patted his spine. "Thanks."

The scholomantic's pleasure flowed through their link.

"So what are we going to practice?"

"As you guessed we're going to work on you sharing your spells with your book. Ordinarily this isn't something we teach freshmen. Not much point since you're technically not allowed to have a familiar until your second year. But in your case we'll have to make an exception. That happens a lot, doesn't it?"

Conryu grinned. "Yeah, but what can we do?"

"Indeed. Ready to begin?"

He spent the next two hours trying to force a Cloak of Darkness spell to cover himself and Prime. After twenty castings Conryu was exhausted and the best he managed was a scattering of black spots so it looked like Prime had a fungus infection.

"That's enough for now," Mrs. Umbra said. "Feel free to practice that as much as you like. By that I mean for at least an hour a day. We meet up again in three days. I expect you to be able to cover both yourself and the book in darkness."

Conryu nodded and stood up. "We'll get there."

* * *

Maria reached the top-floor landing and made the short walk to the light magic classroom. She was eager to find out what they'd be working on this semester. She assumed healing since along with warding it was a light wizard's primary area of expertise. It would be nice to be able to have something concrete to offer Conryu.

She'd told him she doubted she was strong enough to join him on his journey, but if she learned to heal that would be something he couldn't do, even with all his power. That thought made her smile. It was nice to think there was something magical Conryu couldn't accomplish.

Inside the classroom about two-thirds of the others had arrived and were sitting at their desks. Mrs. Alustrial was standing at the front of the class, looking especially stern with her face twisted in a deep scowl. She glared at Maria as she made her way to the desk she shared with Irene.

"What did you do to get on her bad side?" Irene asked.

"No idea. This is the first time I've seen her since midterms. Congratulations on passing by the way."

"Thanks, you too. Shame about Corrie."

"Yeah." Maria hadn't seen the weakest member of their class since she arrived, but the girl had to be upset. If Maria was ever demoted to the lowest rungs of magical study she'd have cried herself to sleep for weeks. Conryu probably would have done backflips, but the odds of him getting demoted were about as good as the sun not rising in the morning.

The last of the class entered with seconds to spare and took their seats. Mrs. Alustrial tapped the chalkboard with her pointer and everyone fell silent.

"Thank you, ladies. For the rest of the year we will be working on healing."

There were murmurs and Maria did a mental fist pump. Healing, just as she'd hoped.

Mrs. Alustrial cleared her throat. "Before we begin I want to discuss what happened at midterms, especially the shameful display by Conryu Koda."

This time the mutters had an angry tone. Everyone had been embarrassed when Conryu had demolished their best work with no visible effort. Maria had been a little annoyed too, but considering the way most people treated him she didn't blame Conryu for showing off a little. Besides, he claimed it was his teacher's idea.

"That sort of showboating has no place in our fine school. I complained to his teacher as well as Dean Blane, but since he didn't break any rules no punishment was levied. Mrs. Lenore even had the gall to note that a little humility would do me... that is, us, good." Mrs. Alustrial started pacing as her face grew red. "As though it were my fault that every year for the past ten years her students haven't been strong enough to defeat my best students. Her bitterness was hardly attractive."

Looked like her teacher had a bruised ego. Talk about not attractive. When her classes first began Maria had looked up to Mrs. Alustrial, now she was starting to wonder.

"So," Mrs. Alustrial continued. "As long as you're in my class you will have no contact with Conryu and as little contact with the rest of the dark magic class as possible. We wouldn't want their negative attitudes rubbing off on you. Understood?"

Maria heard nothing after the order to avoid Conryu. It was ridiculous and she had no right to tell them who they could hang out with after class.

Mrs. Alustrial fixed her gaze on Maria. "I said, understood?"

"No, ma'am, it is not understood. I'm not going to stop seeing my friend just because he upset you and I doubt you have the authority to make me."

The muscle at Mrs. Alustrial's jaw bunched. "As your primary teacher I have all the authority I need. You will avoid that boy even if I have to assign you to detention every free moment you have."

Maria glared back. "I wonder what Dean Blane will have to say?"

"This is not her concern, you will say nothing about it."

"I won't mention your threats if you back off your order to avoid Conryu."

The two women engaged in a staring match for half a minute before Mrs. Alustrial looked away. "Do what you want. But if you need extra help with healing, like you did with wards, I suggest you find someone else to ask."

Bitch!

At this point Maria wouldn't have asked her for help if her life depended on it. It was going to be a long second half of the year.

* * *

After an agreeable dinner with Maria, Conryu headed back to his room. He needed to talk to Mrs. Lenore, but he wasn't sure if he should tell her about Prime. For the moment he'd copy the pages on fusion magic and say Mrs. Umbra gave them to him, which was close enough to the truth.

The moment he stepped into his room the pixie swirled around his neck in wind form, then turned into a tiny girl and settled on his shoulder.

Prime flew out of his grasp and snarled at the pixie. She pressed herself against his cheek and trembled.

"Stop that, Prime. This is the first friend I made when I arrived and I'll not have you scaring her. You two are going to have to learn to get along."

The pixie flew up near the ceiling and stuck her tongue out at Prime. The scholomantic rushed toward her, but Conryu snatched him out of the air. "Enough. Open up to that page about fusion magic so I can copy it."

Prime glared once more at the pixie and landed on his desk, open to the page he needed. It took the better part of an hour for him to copy the three pages of Infernal along with the images. His drawings weren't as nice as the originals, but they got the idea across.

Satisfied with his efforts Conryu stood up and headed for the door. He paused when he reached for the handle and turned back. "I trust you two will behave yourselves while I'm gone."

Prime slammed himself shut on the table while the pixie transformed into wind and blew out of his room. So much the better if they weren't in there alone. Conryu stepped out into the hall and shut the door. It was like trying to keep a pair of angry feral cats apart with those two. They'd only known each other for a day and already seemed to hate one another. Didn't he have enough to worry about?

He put that minor annoyance aside and headed toward Mrs. Lenore's room. It was convenient for him that his teacher was also the dark magic dorm supervisor. She had the center room so no one could claim she played favorites by being closer to one side or the other. He had a hard time imagining that was an issue, but then again he'd heard of stupider things.

Conryu knocked and a moment later Mrs. Lenore opened the door. She'd traded her black robes for soft pink pajamas that draped over a slim, but still curvy figure. He was so surprised he took a step back. Mrs. Lenore slammed the door in his face.

A few seconds later it opened again and she'd thrown her robe over the pajamas. Her cheeks were bright red and she refused to meet his gaze. "Conryu. Can I help you with something?"

Probably best not to mention the PJs. "Yeah. Mrs. Umbra had an idea about the combination magic thing. Is this a good time to talk?"

"Of course, of course, come in." She stepped aside and he went in.

Her room was identical to his, except for some extra decorations. A pair of pink bunny slippers that were a perfect match for the pajamas peeked out from under her bed. He couldn't restrain a smile.

Mrs. Lenore noticed where he was looking, hurried over, and kicked the slippers out of sight. "What did she have to say?"

"Right." Conryu handed her his copied notes. "She thought fusion magic might be the solution to our problem."

She'd barely started looking at the pages when something whistled in the bathroom. "Damn it! My tea."

"I'll get it." He started for the bathroom door.

"No!" She stumbled in her rush to block him.

Conryu didn't know what to do when Mrs. Lenore fell right towards him and in his moment of hesitation their feet tangled up and they ended up in a heap on the floor.

She lifted her head up out of his crotch and offered a shaky smile. "This isn't going very well, is it?"

"Not very. Why don't I sit on the bed and when you're ready we can talk?"

"That's an excellent idea."

They separated and regained a modest amount of decorum. Conryu sat on the edge of the bed while Mrs. Lenore disappeared into the bathroom to deal with the whistling teapot. Why there was a whistling teapot in her bathroom was a subject he didn't want to explore.

A short while later she emerged with a steaming mug. "I'd offer you a drink, but I only have the one cup."

"That's fine. I don't like tea anyway. So, about fusion magic. Do you think that would work?"

She sat beside him and spread out the pages he brought. "I won't lie, I'm not at all familiar with this sort of magic. I've never taught it or even seen it performed. I'm not saying it wouldn't work, but the ritual is so far outside my area of expertise..." She shrugged.

"That's cool. Like you said, I can probably do the final on my own, I was just thinking since we don't have the right number of girls for five-member teams this might be a way for the two odd ones out to work with me. Maybe it would be best to go with six-person teams and me alone."

"No, it won't be." She scrubbed a hand over her face. "Six is too many for such inexperienced wizards. Some of the girls have the skill to pull it off. I think I might go with one group of six and one of five, but that still leaves one girl out."

"I think Kelsie would be willing to work with me on the fusion magic. What do you say I ask her and if she says yes, we give it a try?"

"Can I keep these notes? If it's not too complex I should be able to figure it out in short order, at least enough to help you two. Make sure you tell her she'll have to learn circle casting along with fusion magic so it'll be extra work."

"Will do, thanks. I'll go try and hunt up Kelsie." Conryu started for the door then turned back. "By the way, those are cool slippers."

Mrs. Lenore pointed at the door, but the hint of a smile played around her lips.

* * *

Kelsie didn't have a room of her own. She stayed in a group room with the other freshmen girls on the opposite end of the floor from his suite. This could be awkward if all twelve of his classmates were around. Well, there was nothing for it.

He left Mrs. Lenore's room and made the short walk down to the... barracks? That didn't seem like the right word. Quarters maybe? He sighed and quit trying to distract himself. Going to the girls' room was perfectly innocent and nothing to be concerned about.

Conryu gathered himself outside the door and knocked. A minute later a glowering blond who'd never introduced herself to him opened the door. At least she still had her robe on.

"What?"

"I was looking for Kelsie."

"Why?"

He was half a breath from telling her it was none of her business when Kelsie rushed up to the door. "Conryu. This is a surprise. What brings you here so late?"

He was pretty sure it wasn't that late, but that was beside the point. "I have a proposition for you. Got a minute?"

"Sure, we were just practicing circle casting. Let's take a walk."

They left the still-frowning blond behind and headed back toward his room. He didn't say anything until they were halfway there.

"So I was talking to Mrs. Lenore and we've come up with an idea that will let me team up with someone for the final. It's called fusion casting."

"Never heard of it."

Conryu held his door open for her then closed it behind them. "Basically it does just what it sounds like. One person fuses their power to another's to create a more powerful whole. I haven't gotten too heavily into the details yet, but if you're interested I thought we might team up for the final."

"Absolutely!" Her enthusiasm surprised him for half a second before she added, "If I team up with you there's no way I can fail."

"Before you get too excited I have to tell you that you'll also have to study circle casting. This will make extra work for you."

She waved a hand. "That's fine. One of the things my mom taught me is how to spot a sure thing. You and anything to do with dark magic is a sure thing. I'm in."

"Cool. I'll tell Mrs. Lenore and we can figure out a practice schedule."

Chapter 2

Sunday at School

The rest of the first week went by in a hurry. He divided his time between practicing with Prime and with Kelsie. He could now cover both himself and the scholomantic in a Cloak of Darkness. Mrs. Umbra had them working on a calling spell that would bring Prime to him through a dark portal if they were separated. That trick made the Cloak of Darkness seem like child's play.

When his day off finally arrived it had been a total relief until he remembered he had to visit Angus. Now Conryu found himself approaching the door to the office where they stuck the professor during his visits. The halls were silent in this part of the school, especially on a Sunday.

The office was a little space, barely big enough for the professor and his desk, much less a spare chair and Conryu. It smelled faintly of ammonia and was at the opposite end of the floor from the administrative area. He secretly suspected the so-called office was actually a converted storage closet. Not that he

17

blamed the staff for sticking Angus in a hole in the wall as far from them as they could manage without putting him outside.

The door was open and Conryu poked his head in. "Any news?"

Angus looked up from the book he'd been reading. "Nothing from Chief Kane."

"Cool. See you next week."

"Please, can't you give me just a minute of your time?"

The professor sounded so depressed Conryu stepped into the room. "What is it?"

"Is there nothing I can say to impress upon you how important it is for your story to be told?"

"You don't care about my story. You talk about how you're this big expert, but you don't know shit about wizards, male or female. All you have is a stupid theory that I had the misfortune to prove partially possible and now you've latched on to me like a tapeworm in hopes of making a buck and getting your good name back." Conryu was panting and his face burned. He shouldn't have said anything, but he'd been wanting to get that off his chest for a while.

"Do you really believe that?" Angus sounded genuinely hurt.

"Is there some reason I shouldn't?"

"Come in and sit down." Angus sounded as old as he looked. "Maybe I should tell you my story."

Conryu hesitated then went in. Stupid curiosity. He should just leave, but now he had to know. He squeezed himself into the tiny room and sat on the little plastic chair.

"When I was a boy in Scotland I wasn't the strongest or healthiest, so I spent most of my time at the little library in our village. I think I was twelve when I stumbled on a story about Arthur and Merlin. The wizard fascinated me, haunted me even. I read everything I could find about him and when I ran out of books I went online and did more research. Everything about him was labeled fiction, but I wondered."

"Wondered what?"

"If everyone knew male wizards were impossible, why did someone bother to make up such a character, even for a work of fiction? And it wasn't just Merlin. Many other books featured a male wizard as a character. Why, if it was impossible? I couldn't stop pondering the question. I devoted my life to trying to tease out the answer and I came to one inescapable conclusion: all the male wizards, of which Merlin was the first, were patterned after a real person. I based my efforts around that premise and was roundly mocked, even losing my professorship over it. Then you come along and prove that my theory isn't impossible."

"Lucky me."

"No, lucky me. Don't you understand? If I can figure out how you came to be it might prove the rest of my theory, that Merlin's spirit lingered after death and influenced your birth. I don't know how to prove it, but I have to." Angus's eyes almost glowed with strength of his obsession.

Conryu got up and shook his head. "That's a great story, but your fantasy doesn't interest me. I'm stuck being a wizard. I've made peace with that, more or less. What I'm not willing to be is a research subject. All the teachers already send weekly updates to the Department. I suppose I can be grateful they didn't want to dissect me. I'd thank them for that, but I don't want to give them any ideas. I need to go."

He stood up and headed out, leaving the silently staring professor behind.

* * *

Conryu stalked through the quiet halls in a foul mood. How dare the professor expect him to validate a theory he didn't believe in or understand? The old man's obsession was his problem, not Conryu's. He badly wanted to punch something, but knocking a hole in the wall wouldn't do any good.

He looked around again, but found himself alone in the hall. He took a deep breath and did the first movement of the most basic kata. He worked his way through it, remembering his father's advice and letting the anger flow out of him with each breath.

Angus and his crazy ideas were beyond his influence, just like having to come to this school was beyond his influence. As his body moved through the familiar forms he came to understand that what really made him angry wasn't Angus, but his lack of control, the world's complete indifference to what he wanted.

Once the reason became clear the tension melted away. Instead of fighting he needed to accept his situation. His anger wouldn't change anything. He needed to forget about the future and focus on the moment. If circumstances required him to learn to be a wizard, he'd be the best damn wizard they'd ever seen. After he graduated he could put that all aside and do what he wanted. No one would have any claim on him beyond those he allowed.

He finished the last movement and sighed, his mind clear and focused for maybe the first time since he arrived at this school. He continued down the hall at a quick walk. Maria was probably wondering where he was. His meetings with Angus usually only lasted a minute or two.

He found her pacing in the entryway, arms crossed and scowling. "Sorry I'm late." He leapt down the last four steps.

She stopped and turned to face him. "What took you so long?"

"Angus wanted to tell me his life story and like an idiot I agreed to listen. Kind of pitiful actually."

"So do you know what the dark magic final will be yet?"

"Circle casting. Not for me though. Naturally my power doesn't allow me to do the same thing as the rest of the people in my class. I have to do something called fusion magic. Kelsie and I are teaming up for the final."

"You and Kelsie, huh?"

"Yeah. Remember, no getting jealous. So what about your final?"

"The whole second semester is focused on healing with the final being the construction of a healing ward around a badly injured animal. If it lives we pass, otherwise we fail."

"Ouch, poor critter." She swatted him on the arm. "Hey! I didn't mean yours, but I wouldn't want to be stuck with the girl that failed the midterm."

"Don't worry, Corrie's not going to have to take the final. Once she failed the midterm she was downgraded to basic instruction only. All she'll learn from now on are the simplest universal spells with no further testing."

"Geez, that's rough."

"Yeah, but the theory is if she can't manage the first-year midterm then she doesn't have much hope of learning more advanced techniques. There were seven other girls from the remaining classes that got downgraded with her, so at least Corrie isn't on her own." Maria cocked her head as if listening to something he couldn't hear. "I'm late for alchemy. See you for dinner?"

"You bet."

She kissed him on the cheek and trotted off. One of the older students must have sent a wind spirit to fetch her. Conryu watched her until she was out of sight, enjoying the hints of her figure visible under the flowing white robe. He stretched and yawned. He hadn't spoken to Sonja or the other girls from the golem club so he had no idea if they were still planning to meet up.

He headed for the door. The easiest thing would be to go over and find out for himself. If they were there, great, if not, well, he'd deal with that when he had to.

* * *

They needed to make the robes thicker, or maybe add a fur liner in the winter. Conryu shivered as he quick-stepped down a narrow path through the snowy grounds toward the club's workshop. On days like this he especially missed home. Being right on the ocean Sentinel City never got this cold. Hopefully Sonja would have the shed all heated up when he arrived.

"Do you ever get cold?" He had Prime tucked under one arm like a football.

"No, Master. Demons are much more durable than mortals. Only magical cold causes me any discomfort."

"Lucky you."

As he walked he kept his head on a swivel. Everyone was holed up inside where it was warm so if someone wanted to try something this would be an ideal time. He hadn't been attacked in months, not that he was complaining, but he also doubted the people that wanted him dead had simply given up. Every day that went by without an event made him even more nervous.

"Shit!"

The shed was closed up tight, no steam rose from the roof, and no tracks marred the snow in front of the door. Where was everyone? He scratched his head and began to retrace his steps.

Why had he imagined anyone would be there in the first place? The Brawl had come and gone, so they didn't really have anything to work towards. Maybe he'd been foolish to think someone would let him know, but he found it annoying all the same.

He had only gone a few paces when an explosion shook the ground. It wasn't coming from nearby and he dismissed the notion of an attack at once. A second, larger blast caused the snow to fall from some nearby trees.

"Reveal." He scanned the area and soon spotted magical energy coming from down by the lake. All the elements were represented.

Curiosity and cold warred within him before curiosity won. He jogged toward the lake and several hundred yards later the trees opened up, revealing a gathering of several hundred students. Conryu paused at what he considered a safe distance and watched the proceedings.

A girl in blue-green robes stood at the edge of the lake and waved her hands. He was too far away to make out what she was saying, but soon a dragon made of water rose up out of the lake. Another girl, this one in black, assumed the position for Dispel. A black orb shot out and struck the dragon. Another boom sounded as the mass of water splashed down in the lake.

He didn't know what sort of test they were taking and he didn't especially care. Conryu rushed back to the dorm and went down to his room. Inside it was nice and warm. A hot, dry breeze swirled around him, driving the cold out. When he was nice and toasty the pixie settled on his shoulder. Prime flew over and landed on his desk, apparently too cold to even muster a growl for the little wind spirit. So much for the durability of demons.

What was he supposed to do now? He could practice summoning Prime, but he'd been looking forward to a break from magic. He turned to look at the pixie, who smiled at him.

"Do you know Sonja Chard? She's a senior, fire wizard, came to visit me a few weeks back."

She hung her head and gave it a shake. A moment later she perked up and whistled something in the piping language of the wind.

Conryu sighed. "I don't understand."

She stared at him for a handful of seconds then turned into a breeze and blew out the door. Maybe he offended her.

"Pixies are flighty creatures." Prime flew up off the desk. "A random thought probably popped into her empty little head and she flitted off to explore it."

"Why do you dislike her so much? As far as I can tell she's an absolute sweetheart yet you've done nothing but growl and snap at her since we got here."

Prime flexed his cover in what Conryu had come to recognize as his approximation of a human shrug. "I'm a demon."

He said it like that was the only explanation required. "Would you care to elaborate?"

"Demons and other spirits have never gotten along. Just being in their presence makes my pages crawl. I can barely tolerate the wind spirit and the water spirit peeking at us from the bathroom."

Conryu turned his head just in time to catch a glimpse of the naiad vanishing out of the doorway.

"But only because you command it, Master. To put it simply, demons do not play well with others."

"Great."

The pixie blew back in and turned into a girl. She grabbed his robe and tugged him toward the door. He started to ask what she was doing before he remembered he wouldn't understand even if she told him. Conryu held out his hand and Prime flew into it, shifting as he went so he resembled an especially ugly leather-bound book.

"I'm coming."

He followed her up and out of the basement, down the long hall to the cafeteria. Sonja sat by herself in an ill-lit corner, a bag of vanilla cookies on the table in front of her. She nibbled one with a distant look on her face.

"You found her for me, thanks."

The pixie rubbed her cheek against his and blew away.

Now he had to figure out why Sonja looked so depressed. Conryu had always favored the direct approach so he walked over, laid Prime on the table, and sat across from her. "Hey."

Sonja looked up at him. She had dark ridges under her eyes. "Go away."

He grabbed the bag of cookies out from under her nose. "Can't do that. There's a new rule: depressed people aren't allowed to eat cookies, it just brings the rest of us down and insults the cookies."

He grabbed one and popped it in his mouth. It was dry, bland, and way too sweet. Why on earth did she favor the nasty things?

"I refuse to be cheered up. Now give me my cookies and leave me alone."

"At the very least you owe me an explanation. I half froze on my way out to the shed. And when I arrived, instead of my favorite fire wizard, I find a closed door and not so much as a note."

She reached for the cookies, but he pulled them further back. "If you're a good girl and tell me why the only club that would let me join has disbanded I'll let you have one."

"There's no point to meeting anymore. The Brawl's over and I'm graduating this summer. I am sorry I forgot to tell you."

"So, what, you're going to spend the rest of your Sundays alone in the cafeteria moping and eating cookies?"

"That was my plan."

"Fine, but if we're going to mope we are going to do it properly. Just a minute." Conryu went over to the kitchen and bought a pair of ice cream cups and grabbed two spoons. He opened one and set it in front of Sonja. "There. According to my mom you can't have a proper mope without ice cream. Now, do you want to eat in silence or do you want to tell me about it?"

Sonja grabbed a cookie, nibbled it, and blew out a sigh. "It's my family. They want me to come work for them as soon as I graduate. I love my parents, but I really don't want to work at the factory."

"Did you tell them?" Conryu took a bite of ice cream. Much better than the cookies.

"No. They were so excited about me joining the company I didn't have the heart. I don't know what to do. If I tell them I want to work with them I'll be miserable and if I tell them I don't I'll feel like a shit-heel. It's your classic no-win situation."

Sounded like Sonja had the same problem as Kelsie. Did anyone have a good relationship with their parents besides Conryu and Maria? "Do you get along with your parents?"

"Oh, yeah. They're great, a little workaholic maybe, but otherwise great. I never planned on working with them you know. I was going to go into engineering, but senior year I passed the wizards' test with a decent score and they immediately began planning how I could help out. It was like they forgot I had other plans."

Conryu smiled, thinking of his own plans, now on hold. A burst of inspiration struck. "You ever think about building a motorcycle with an engine that runs on magic?"

She stared at him. "Why would anyone build an engine that ran on magic? A gas engine is much simpler."

"Just to see if it was possible. You'd need earth magic to make the parts move. Water magic for lubrication."

"No, earth magic would handle that as well, oil comes from the earth after all. You could use fire magic for extra thrust and wind magic to keep the bugs out of your teeth."

"What about something for safety?" He took another bite of his ice cream and struggled not to smile.

"The wind bubble could probably handle that too." She dropped her cookie and frowned at him. "I know what you're trying to do and it won't work. I'm determined to be miserable."

"Right. Do you think fire magic in the combustion chamber would work better than earth magic to power the engine?"

The discussion lasted for another hour and by the end he doubted he could have kept Sonja from trying to build a magic engine even if he wanted to. "Do you think Crystal, Onyx, and Jade would be interested in working on it?"

"Crystal for sure, as long as she doesn't make the academy team. The others were pretty pissed when I closed up shop so they may have moved on."

"Wait, the academy team? You mean for the Four Nations' Tournament?"

"Yeah, they're holding tryouts today down by the lake. Crystal wanted to give it a shot, but I don't think she can beat the earth magic wizard from last year's team. Crystal will be a senior next year and the current girl will have graduated so she should have a good chance if she wants to try again."

"Why didn't you try out?" Conryu asked. "You're pretty strong in fire magic."

"One of the girls in my grade is way stronger than me and she's trying out. I'd have no chance against her."

"Oh, well, we'll just have to focus on the engine. I can handle the repairs if you two take care of the magic. It shouldn't be hard to lay my hands on a motor and tools. Shall we get started next week?"

"Might as well. We're out of cookies and ice cream." She jumped up, ran around the table, and hugged him. "Thanks. This should be fun."

He grinned, thrilled at the prospect of working on a motor again, and even more thrilled to see Sonja back to her usual self.

* * *

Lady Mockingbird's heels clicked on the stairs as she led her four strongest girls down to the basement casting chamber. She'd spent her every free moment the past week poring over the research notes taken from the Kincade's lab. She'd never admit it, but some of the magical theory was way over her head and she considered herself well read when it came to advanced wizardry.

Nevertheless she felt confident that she understood the process sufficiently to begin the summoning and binding portion of the project. She would, however, be taking all necessary precautions, thus the line of girls following with bowed heads.

At the bottom of the steps she turned left and entered the austere casting chamber. Everything had been removed, even her full-length scrying mirror, to be certain no stray magic would interfere with her casting and to protect the valuable item from out-of-control spirits.

Following the directions in the lab notes, she'd spent hours after her classes inscribing a spell circle. The complex mix of runes intertwined and covered most of the floor. She had to be careful not to stare as the runes had a tendency to twist and writhe in her vision, filling her with nausea and a hint of vertigo.

"Places, ladies." She'd gone over the project often enough that the four girls hurried to the four corners of the room and settled in to await her next command.

Lady Mockingbird stepped to the center of the circle and placed the jar at her feet before tiptoeing back, careful not to disturb any of her delicate runes. She would start with fire as that was her strongest element.

She threw her hands up and to the sides, a dramatic and unnecessary gesture, but one that pleased her nonetheless. This was a moment to savor, the moment when Conryu Koda's life ended and her ascension to Hierarch became reality.

"Begin."

The girls chanted the same spell, each in the language of their aligned element. Lines of energy climbed the walls and ceiling; red, white, brown, and blue intertwined and fused, creating a massive protective barrier around the chamber.

When all the lines had appeared and the girls had fallen into a monotonous, sustained chant, Lady Mockingbird began her summoning. "From the hottest realm I call you, child of fire. Appear and serve a loyal ally of flame. Fire Summoning!" The power built slowly as the heat in the room rose. Sweat drenched her body, running down her back and legs, and soaking her red robe.

She ignored all the distractions, focusing on her will and desire. A flaming gate appeared in the middle of the chamber directly above the jar. She called the name of a spirit well known to her. "Azoth Blazewing."

It was a shame to sacrifice such a valuable servant, but she wanted to be certain her first summoning went smoothly and the blazewing was of sufficient power for her needs.

The flames shifted and swirled before a shining, translucent wing emerged, followed by a second. The moment they cleared the flames the wings beat so fast they became a blur. Wind rushed around Lady Mockingbird, drying the sweat for a moment.

A dragonfly as long as she was tall pulled itself free of the portal. The moment the blazewing cleared the gate she collapsed it. The giant, flaming insect zipped around the room a couple times before hovering in front of Lady Mockingbird.

She crooned to it in the language of fire, soothing the spirit's distress. With gentle coaxing she positioned it directly above the Chimera Jar. She offered it a gentle smile and spoke the activation phrase for the artifact. "Make many into one."

Black tentacles shot up out of the mouth of the jar and dragged the blazewing down. It buzzed and spat flames, all to no avail. A minute later it was gone and the temperature of the room had dropped back to normal.

Lady Mockingbird wiped her brow. One down, three to go. "Take five, ladies."

The students fell silent and slumped against the wall. They'd done well. None of her girls had faltered when the blazewing appeared nor had they fumbled a single word during the lengthy summoning. She expected no less, but was still pleased that they met her high standards.

Ten minutes later, when the girls had caught their breaths and her strength had returned enough to resume, Lady Mockingbird clapped her hands. "Positions."

They all scrambled up and restored the wards. When they'd fallen into a comfortable rhythm she chanted in the language of earth. It was essentially the same spell only in a different language. As a fire wizard Lady Mockingbird knew far fewer earth spirits than she did fire, but one whose name she'd found in her research should closely match the blazewing in power.

The lab notes had been very definite that all four spirits used in the chimera had to be of like power. That was why she used the blazewing instead of one of the more powerful fire spirits she'd met over the years.

The floor rumbled as the spell reached its conclusion and the earth portal opened. She called the name of the spirit. "Prima Basilisk." A moment later the knobby, horned head of the basilisk emerged from the gate. It dragged itself into the chamber using eight heavily muscled legs that ended in talons as long as her forearm.

The basilisk turned its yellow gaze on Lady Mockingbird and loosed a roar that shook the chamber. She ended the spell, closing the gate and trapping the earth lizard in their reality. Unlike the blazewing, the basilisk didn't look on her with a gentle expression.

Though earth and fire got along most of the time, summoning the beast into the close confines of the casting chamber put the basilisk on its guard and her at a disadvantage. She couldn't give it time to attack. It had appeared close enough to the jar that she risked speaking the activation phrase.

The tentacles shot out again, and the ends flailed against the basilisk's pebbly hide. Damn it! The earth spirit was just out of range.

Lady Mockingbird raised a hand. "Burn my enemies to ash. Flame Blast!" A jet of fire streaked toward the basilisk. Her spell splashed against its tough skin, but instead of driving it closer to the jar it only enraged the beast.

The basilisk roared, lowered its head, and charged toward the wall. The house trembled, but the wards held.

Many more blows like that and the building wouldn't survive. Even from a distance the tension on the face of the girl protecting that wall was clear. One more solid hit would knock her out.

Lady Mockingbird chanted another spell. "Flames of protection!" A wall of flames shot up between the basilisk and the wall it had just struck. The beast shook its head and turned toward her. It wasn't the brightest creature in existence, but it had just enough intelligence to recognize her as the source of its problems.

It snarled and charged right at her. Its crest horn looked far bigger when it was pointed right at her chest. A quick wind spell empowered her leap and carried her over the beast's back. She whistled once in midair to adjust her trajectory, avoiding the flailing tentacles and coming to a safe landing on the opposite side of the jar.

The basilisk slammed full speed into the wall behind her last position, shaking the building and making the wards tremble. If she couldn't force it into the jar soon she'd have to send it back to its home dimension or risk losing the building.

It turned to face her and she dared hope it might be stupid enough to charge right through the tentacles in its rage to reach her.

That hope was thwarted when it stalked to the left, keeping well away from the jar. At least it hadn't decided to attack one of the girls. If even one of them lost her focus the wards would collapse allowing the basilisk to smash its way out with ease.

The basilisk didn't have the right sort of magic to read her mind, but as it passed one of the girls its tail lashed out. The casual blow couldn't penetrate the barrier, but it startled the young wizard enough that she stammered through a portion of the chant.

The line of energy fluctuated and collapsed. Dumb though it was, the basilisk was still a magical creature. Its head perked up the moment the wards collapsed.

It was no use. Lady Mockingbird chanted the portal spell again, this time opening it right under the beast's many feet. It fell through the opening and back into its own realm. She sealed the gate, not giving it a chance to climb back out. Another quick incantation deactivated the jar.

Though she hated to admit it, even to herself, Lady Mockingbird was going to need some help if she wanted to secure the remaining spirits required to complete the chimera.

Chapter 3

Sentinel Search

Terra slowly coaxed the residual energy out of the open box and away from the blob of necroplasma. She'd turned off every light save one in the casting chamber to minimize distractions. She'd been fiddling with the ugly blob since Conryu opened the box for them. Every trick she'd tried failed to coax it to do anything but slam itself over and over again into the containment circle. She'd finally given up and returned to her original plan of determining the purpose of the artifact once contained in the box.

The cloud of dark energy rose above the blob and when it was high enough she opened a small gap in the containment field and brought it out. She breathed a sigh of relief when the energy cleared the opening and the field had resealed. Though she had absolutely no experience dealing with necroplasma, Terra didn't want her first effort to be chasing the mad blob all over her casting chamber.

Now that she didn't have to divide her focus Terra used wisps of dark energy to nudge the cloud of energy into its former shape, using the fragmented lines running through it as a guide. It was a tedious task combining optimism and guesswork.

Hours passed, or so she assumed from the stiffness in her back, but at last the final line fell into place. Her heart skipped a beat when she recognized what the spell did. The five artifacts would tap into the power of the floating island to open multiple portals to the netherworld to summon god knew how many shadow beasts into the city. If it worked tens of thousands might die.

At least now she knew why nothing had happened since the battle with the bikers and the theft of their bodies. Mercia couldn't trigger the summoning until the island returned this summer. That was their one advantage. If they somehow located and destroyed the boxes before the island returned, Mercia's plan would fail. If even one remained she could still summon dozens of monsters capable of killing scores or more people.

That was beyond contemplation.

The cloud of energy dissipated and she switched the lights back on. The blob appeared less energetic when she left the room fully lit.

She strode out of the chamber and down the hall to Lin's office. Hopefully he'd finished mapping the potential hiding places. She paused outside the unmarked door, knocked once, adjusted her hair and robe, and pushed it open.

Lin sat behind his desk hunched over a cheap laptop, the pile of notes beside him. He looked up and smiled. "Hey. Any progress?"

"Some." She told him what she'd discovered and when she finished Lin stared at her, his mouth hanging open.

"You're saying she could summon hundreds of creatures like those things that attacked Conryu? How would we even begin to deal with something like that?"

"If it happens, all the wizards in the city wouldn't be enough to stop every shadow beast before it killed someone. We need to handle this before the island returns. Have you finished mapping all the potential hiding spots?"

"All the ones the computer and I could come up with." He typed a command and an aerial map of the city appeared on the screen. Hundreds of little red dots littered it.

"Can you overlay the path of the floating island?"

Another command produced a wide gray path over the city.

"You can eliminate anything outside of that swath."

Dozens of little dots vanished, leaving far too many behind. Lin hung his head. "That's still a hell of a lot of spots to check."

"She'll want to open the portals in the most densely populated part of the city, so you can eliminate everything outside the city center."

"Okay, that leaves around sixty left to check. That's a lot, but manageable. If we deploy the city police we should be able to clear the lot of them in a week."

Terra shook her head. "We'll need to send wizards. Mercia will have hidden the boxes behind illusions and magical defenses. If you send regular cops and they trigger a trap... No, that might be almost as bad as a portal opening."

"So, you and me, maybe Clair and the security guy...Adam, right? If we can coax the police into loaning us the department wizard she could check a few locations."

"That should work. Once we find one box I can calculate the approximate location of the other four. I'll round up Clair, you call your former boss. We'll meet downstairs in an hour. Oh, and be sure to print out a list of all the addresses."

* * *

Lin guided the car through the early afternoon traffic. After months of frustration they were finally close to cracking the case. In the time since his reassignment he'd had more than a few doubts about whether they'd ever make any progress, or if Mercia was too clever for them. He never should have doubted Terra. That woman had determination to spare. Though if he never had to look at that list of descriptions again that would be okay.

Beside him Terra stared out the window. They were still a ways from the park where they hoped to find the first box, so he doubted she'd detect anything. Maybe she was mentally preparing herself for whatever they'd have to deal with. Lin felt far out of his depth most days at his new job. Sometimes it came as a relief that they'd just stuck him in an office with his packet of clues. If he'd had to comment on some magical matter he'd have sounded like an idiot.

The light turned red, forcing him to ease to a stop. He glanced at Terra again. She seemed to be in her own world.

He enjoyed the profile of her face and neck for a moment then said, "What's on your mind?"

She jumped as though she'd forgotten he was there. "I was thinking about the warehouse and what sort of trouble we might find when we track down the rest of the boxes."

Lin grimaced. It had been a near thing last summer when he accidentally triggered magic protecting the box they recovered. Only Terra's power had allowed them to escape with their lives, though she'd paid a high price for the effort.

"Maybe it won't be that bad."

"Wishful thinking. Mercia has had months to prepare her defenses and unlike the first one we found, these boxes still have their artifacts inside. No, if all we encounter is a swarm of shadow ravens I'll consider us lucky indeed."

Lin tried to think of something encouraging, but the light changed forcing him to focus on the road. That was probably just as well. Only inane words of encouragement came to mind and she'd see right through them.

Five minutes later he pulled into a space beside the park. It was only half-hour parking, but his government plates should keep them from getting a ticket. He waited for a break in the traffic, climbed out, and joined Terra on the sidewalk.

The park only covered four blocks and according to his research had a single fountain. If the information the biker left was accurate, then the box had to be near it.

"What should I do?"

Terra took her magic-enhancing glasses from a pocket of her gray robe and slid them on. "Just keep your eyes peeled and don't touch anything."

He laughed. "Don't worry, I learned my lesson."

The air was bitter as they walked down the path toward the fountain. The bare branches of the trees cast a spiderweb of shadows across the trail. Lin was glad he had on his heavy wool jacket. He assumed Terra used some sort of magic to keep the air around her warm as her robe seemed far too thin for the weather.

One advantage of the cold, it kept all the people inside and out of their way. If this went sideways, the fewer people around the better.

Terra muttered under her breath as they walked, her gaze flicking back and forth. He doubted they'd find anything this far from the fountain, but she appeared to be taking no chances.

They spent the better part of ten minutes at their deliberate pace to reach the center of the park. Some kids had built a pair of snowmen off to one side. The fountain was a simple octagon of gray stone about hip high and filled with ice. He wanted to draw his pistol, but there was no threat visible and he doubted it would be much use against anything they might encounter.

Terra strode over to the fountain, her chanting rising in volume as she worked her way around it. She examined the sides and top before making a mystical pass that evaporated the ice to allow a better view inside the bowl.

Finally she fell silent and turned to face him. "This place is a bust. There's not even a hint of magic."

Lin shrugged. It was too much to hope they'd hit it on the first try. "Shall we head to the next one?"

They had barely gotten in the car when Terra's phone rang. "Clair? You did? We're on our way."

"What is it?" Lin fired up the car and cranked the heater.

"They found one of the boxes. Clair says it's warded six ways from Sunday and her magic can't touch it. She wants me to come over and lend a hand."

"What's the address?"

* * *

Terra spotted Clair and Adam outside the door of an abandoned building. The sign over the door said "for sale by owner," but there was no name or number written on it. The derelict building sat between an apartment complex and a minimart. A trickle of people eyed the unusual pair loitering around the old building as they made their way up and down the street, but no one took the time to talk.

Lin pulled in behind Clair and Adam's car and they climbed out. Terra marched straight over to Clair. "What did you find?"

"You'd best have a look yourself." Terra followed her inside.

Beyond the door was a large open space covered in graffiti and littered with cigarette butts and empty beer bottles. It looked like the local youth used the place as a hangout. If they couldn't do something about the box, they'd have to make sure no one entered the building.

Clair pointed to a spot on the wall near the ceiling. Terra slipped on her glasses. "Reveal."

A section of the wall shimmered in her enhanced vision and revealed a cutout. A wooden crate sat below the opening. When she climbed up for a better look Terra flinched. A web of dark magic filled the space, the black box barely visible through all the threads.

"Not screwing around, is she?" Terra asked as she climbed back down.

"No. I cast my best breaking spell and it didn't even draw a twitch from the wards. Even together I doubt we'd penetrate it."

"I agree. And even if we did we couldn't open the box itself."

"So what do we do?" Clair sounded nervous and Terra didn't blame her. Despite the evidence it was hard to square what they knew of Mercia from her time at the Department with what she'd accomplished here.

"We need to set up stakeouts at all five locations. If Mercia comes to check on her handiwork they could potentially follow her back to wherever she's hiding out."

"That's a pretty thin plan. She can trigger the spells from anywhere. And whatever else she is, Mercia isn't an idiot. No way she'd do anything to compromise her hiding places or headquarters."

"All true." Terra ran a hand through her hair. "Maybe we should just cordon off the place to keep the locals out. I doubt anyone would bother this box given its location and the illusion hiding it, but if they got to partying and smashing stuff you never know what might happen."

"What do you think, an aversion ward around the building? That should keep any non-wizards out of the area, and if it's broken, it will give us warning that something was happening."

"Good call. Can you handle it? I want to try and figure out where the remaining boxes are most likely hidden."

"No sweat." Clair limbered up her fingers.

Terra left Clair to her casting and walked out of the building. Adam and Lin stood on either side of the door, hands thrust into pockets and steam coming out their mouths. The poor guys were way out of their depths and she felt bad reducing them to chauffeurs and bodyguards. Not bad enough to send them home. It was pretty handy to have someone good with a gun if they should run into any of the more corporeal undead.

"So what's the deal?" Lin asked. "Can you two handle it or not?"

"Definitely not. Clair's going to fix it so the local kids can't go in there anymore. Let's see if we can figure out where the other four are hiding."

"I'm up for anything that gets me out of this cold."

While Lin started the car and cranked up the heat Terra turned to Adam. "She won't be long if you want to wait in your car."

Adam shook his head. "I'll guard the door until she comes out. How are we going to resolve this crisis, Terra?"

Terra offered a tired smile. "When I figure that out, you'll be one of the first to know."

Adam grunted.

Terra climbed into the car beside Lin who already had his computer open and the map on the screen. He highlighted their current location and marked it "number one." "Now what?"

"Eliminate anything further from this point than the diameter of the island."

Lin typed and over half the remaining points vanished. Terra studied them. It didn't take long, using the one position they'd confirmed as a starting point to find the four points that completed a pentagram.

She pointed them out one by one and Lin highlighted them. "It seems so simple now," he said.

"Getting rid of ninety percent of the false locations helped a lot." Clair tapped on the window and she rolled it down. "All done?"

"Yup. Anyone getting too close will have an overwhelming urge to puke their guts out. That ought to convince them to party somewhere else. How about you?"

Lin turned the laptop to show Clair what they'd discovered.

"Standard pentagram layout, nice. You want to ward the other four like I did this one?"

Terra nodded. "For now that's all we can do. Which ones do you want?"

Clair shrugged so Terra gave her the two closest, a church and a funeral home. "Shouldn't take more than an hour or two. We'll have to update the chief when we're finished."

Terra sighed. "Yes. He's not going to be thrilled with our results."

"I'm not thrilled with our results."

Terra couldn't argue with that.

* * *

"Well the clue was right," Lin said as he pulled the car off the access road and parked beside a chain link fence. "It's certainly dark and wet."

They were approaching the location of the final box, a culvert seven feet in diameter that directed storm runoff to the ocean. This was the one he was looking forward to the least. He'd fished more than one body out of these drains over his years on the force.

Lin slid out of the car and shivered. Sunset wasn't for another two hours, but the temperature was dropping already. He walked around the car and joined Terra beside a gate in the fence. It had a padlock of course, but a wave of Terra's hand combined with a muttered command popped it open in a jiffy.

It was a short walk from the gate to the culvert. A wide, concrete gully funneled water from all over the city to this drain. More than one person had drowned over the years when they were caught in a flash flood. One good thing about doing this in the winter was they didn't have to worry about a flood. Pneumonia, on the other hand, seemed a distinct possibility.

"How about sharing a little magical heat over here?"

Terra glanced at him like she'd forgotten he was even there. "Sorry."

She put her hand on his back and warmth flooded through him, drawing a long sigh. "Thanks."

"No problem. Let's get moving. We don't want to do this after dark."

"No, but we have over an hour of daylight and we don't want to slip and break our necks."

The warning proved apt. You could hardly take a step across the snow-covered concrete without hitting a hidden patch of ice. Lin feared he really would break his neck before they reached the culvert.

An iron ladder hammered into the stone granted access to the drainage gully. Lin eyed it and frowned. The black opening of the culvert gave off a bad vibe. "I don't suppose you can ward it from here?"

"Afraid not. First we have to confirm the box is actually down there. Just because we got the other locations right is no guarantee on this one."

"Come on."

"We have to be sure. If it makes you feel better I'll hold your hand when we reach the dark part." She whistled and hopped off the edge of the gully. Terra drifted like a leaf in a breeze to the icy floor.

Must be nice.

He crawled down the ladder, testing each rung as he went. When he reached the bottom his hands ached from the tight grip he'd held on the freezing rungs.

"Shit! I left my flashlight in the car."

Terra hissed and waved a hand. A handful of fire orbs flashed into being. "I think we can manage with these."

She gestured and the balls of flame flew into the culvert opening. Icicles hung from the top and a foot-wide path of brown ice ran down the center. He really didn't want to know what was mixed with that water. At least the cold held down the stink.

He blew out a breath and marched toward the opening, determined to complete the job as quickly as possible. He'd barely taken three steps when Terra grabbed his arm.

"What?"

"Something's not right. The dark magic feels different here, less contained."

Lin reached for his pistol, taking his time, waiting for her to reassure him that it wouldn't be necessary. Terra remained silent, her focus on the still-hidden recesses of the culvert. That told him all he needed to know about the seriousness of the situation.

The flaming orbs drifted deeper into the culvert. He caught a glimpse of pasty white skin and yellow teeth then the moans rang out.

"Aim for the head," Terra said. "I need to stop the overflow of energy so you'll have to deal with the zombies."

"Right." He worked the slide, putting a bullet in the chamber.

Terra whistled and flew up into the leaden sky.

"Hey!"

"Draw them away from the entrance so I can get inside. You'll be fine, zombies are slow."

"Great," he muttered. "Zombies are slow. That's her big piece of wisdom."

The first of the undead shambled out of the culvert and into the light. It was an ugly thing; most of its face had been eaten by rats. Where there had once been eyes there were only black pits.

Lin drew a bead on its head, then lowered his weapon. She wanted them away from the opening, so dropping the first one a step away from it wasn't the best plan. He waved his arms. "Hey, you ugly fucks. Come and get me."

The lead zombie oriented on him and picked up the pace, speeding up to a quick walk.

Lin backpedaled, maintaining the distance between them. One after another walking corpses emerged from the culvert until five of the hideous things were chasing after him in a slow-motion race.

When they were a hundred feet up the gully he put a bullet in the forehead of the closest zombie. It collapsed like a puppet with its strings cut.

But only for a moment. The zombie sat up and the hole in its head closed as he stared in horror.

This was going to be harder than he thought.

* * *

When the first zombie Lin shot sat back up Terra stared in disbelief. When he dropped a second one and it climbed to its feet again she knew she had to hurry. They were far enough up the gully now that she could land without fear.

She conjured more flaming spheres and surrounded herself with a light magic barrier. With her defenses in place she landed and eased her way into the culvert. Behind her more shots rang out.

The zombies were drawing power from the energies of the box and using it to heal wounds that should have destroyed them. Until she sealed that leak Lin couldn't defeat them.

Terra positioned her flame spheres every ten feet as she made her way deeper into the cold darkness. There was really nowhere to hide anything in the culvert, it was just a metal tube with no shelves or hollow walls. She couldn't imagine Mercia simply tossing the box on the ground. A flood would wash it out into the ocean.

Something moved at the edge of her light. She pointed and a flame sphere flew toward it.

"Ugh." She gagged and put her hand over her mouth and nose.

A lumpen mass of flesh sat off to one side of the culvert. Pale, putrefied, and covered in bristly hair, once upon a time it might have been a pig. Deep, slowly regenerating gouges covered the thing. In the center of the mass sat the box.

Disgusting as it was, all she needed to do was conjure a sealing circle around the mass. That should weaken the zombies enough for Lin to finish them off.

"Mine," a guttural, inhuman voice said. From behind the mass an emaciated, hunched-over figure emerged. It had an elongated jaw filled with enough teeth to do a shark proud. A foot-long slime-covered tongue flicked from side to side.

The ghoul ripped a hunk of flesh from the lump with a taloned hand and stuffed it into its dripping mouth. "Mine," it said as it slunk closer.

Terra threw a hand out. "Flames of destruction incinerate my enemy, Fire Blast!" A searing jet of flame shot out.

The ghoul lunged to one side, faster than she expected. The stink of seared flesh indicated that she hadn't missed altogether.

It circled around her, forcing Terra to spin to keep it in sight.

"Fire Blast!"

It dodged a second jet of flames then a third. It was too quick for such an imprecise spell.

She switched to wind magic. "Father of winds lend this unworthy fire wizard the gift of your protection, Tornado Trap!"

A small tornado lifted the ghoul up and smashed it into the top of the culvert, pinning it in place.

She raised a hand. Now that she had it trapped she couldn't miss.

Something snaked around her ankle and yanked her off her feet. The impact broke her concentration and the ghoul fell to the floor.

A fleshy tentacle from the pile of ghoul food had her by the ankle. The light barrier kept it from hurting her, but it was pulling her closer.

Behind her the ghoul's talons scrabbled against steel as it climbed to its feet.

Terra pointed at the tentacle and hissed. A dart of flame severed it six inches from her foot. She rolled over, cupped her hands, and chanted. "Flood the world with flames, Fire Surge!" A river of flames gushed from her hands and roared into the ghoul's mouth. Its head exploded in a shower of gore.

She sighed and climbed to her feet. More shots rang out.

Right, Lin was counting on her. A piece of the ghoul's skull had landed on her shoe. It slid off and worked its way toward the unmoving body. Other pieces were doing the same. Even with its head completely destroyed the ghoul was trying to heal.

She needed to focus. At the rate it was recovering she had maybe five minutes to complete the sealing spell. That should be plenty. Hopefully.

Terra raised her hands and began to chant in Angelic. "Seal the darkness, bind the evil." Glowing runes appeared one after another around the flesh heap. She chanted the phrase over and over as she circled the fleshy mass and drew runes with her fingers.

It extruded more pseudopods and sent one flying at her.

Terra stepped to the side and kept casting. She couldn't break her rhythm or the warding would fail and she'd have to start over.

She crouched down to avoid another attack. The circle was halfway complete.

Two tentacles shot at her this time. Terra dodged one and took a grazing blow to the ribs from the other. She ignored the pain and kept going.

Four tentacles formed. No way to dodge all those and continue the spell.

She had to finish first. Terra picked up the pace of her casting, risking a mistaken enunciation.

The last syllable fell from her lips a moment before the first tentacle shot out. It slammed into her barrier, but failed to smash through.

Good.

She turned to the ghoul and found the remaining pieces of its broken skull had stopped moving.

Shots rang out in quick succession then there was silence. Terra stumbled toward the entrance to the culvert. Lin still needed her.

She stepped into the fading sunlight. Lin was walking toward her, tucking his pistol back into his shoulder holster. He was okay.

Thank god.

* * *

"So after I finished warding the culvert Lin called the police to retrieve the bodies and we came straight back here."

Terra finished her report leaving Orin with a pounding headache. He'd been sitting in his office all day drinking coffee and waiting for news. Now that he had the news the waiting didn't seem so bad. At least Terra and Lin hadn't been seriously injured in the confrontation.

Clair had given her report half an hour ago. She and Adam hadn't run into any monsters, but neither of his wizards had been remotely successful in dealing with the actual problem. He shouldn't have been surprised given how ineffective they'd been with the first box, but it was still a disappointment.

"So what do you suggest we do about it? Your wards won't stop Mercia from activating the artifacts when the island returns, will they?"

"No, they're very simple defenses designed to keep ordinary citizens from wandering into a dangerous location." Terra slumped in her chair. "We need to call him back. There's simply no other option."

"You realize how it looks, the Department of Magic having to rely on a first-year academy student to solve our problems for us?"

"It looks terrible, but given the alternative..." She shrugged.

There it was. That simple, exhausted shrug spoke volumes. However much Orin would have liked to spare Conryu any more trouble, he had no choice. With the northern incursion stretching their wizards thin, he had to rely on the assets available.

"Do you think we could wrap it up in a day?"

"With Conryu's power he could break the wards in an afternoon, but that assumes no traps are activated when he does. I have no certainties to offer you save one. If we do nothing, on June 25 the city will be flooded with nether spirits. Enough that it will probably take every wizard the Department can muster to destroy them all and even then I'd expect massive casualties."

"I'll call Dean Blane and make the arrangements. If we can bring him in Sunday morning and get him back before classes on Monday, no one will even need to know about the threat. The last thing we need is to start a panic."

Chapter 4

Chaos on Sunday

Another Sunday had rolled around, once more forcing Conryu to make the walk to Angus's dinky office to check in. Conryu's mind was a million miles away. Who would have thought it would be so difficult to find an engine? Everyone he asked turned him down. Over and over the same thing: it was against the no technology rule. He wanted to turn it into a magic item, but that didn't do much to convince them. It looked like his experiment was going to end before it began.

Sonja would be so disappointed. She'd really been looking forward to the project, so had he for that matter. He really hoped the professor didn't feel the need to share any more of his life story. He didn't have the patience for it today.

Conryu adjusted his grip on the scholomantic. Despite another two weeks of practice he still hadn't managed to summon Prime through a portal yet. Mrs. Umbra assured him that it was the most complex thing he'd attempted so far and he shouldn't be disappointed if he couldn't master it right away.

He frowned when he reached Angus's office. The door was closed tight. Usually he left it open until Conryu arrived.

Conryu's knock was met with a quick, "Come in."

He pushed the door open and stuck his head in. Dean Blane was sitting in his chair.

"Get in here and shut the door," she said.

He complied at once, shutting the door tight. "What—"

She pressed a finger to her lips. When he fell silent she cast a spell in the whispery language of the wind. "Okay, we can talk now."

"What's going on?"

Dean Blane took a breath, but Angus cleared his throat before she spoke. "Fine, you tell him."

"Thank you." Angus smoothed the front of his tweed jacket. "I have a message from Chief Kane. You're needed back in Sentinel City. The rest of the boxes have been located and you're the only one strong enough to break the wards protecting them. Isn't this wonderful? People are already starting to recognize how special you are."

Conryu resisted the almost overwhelming urge to punch Angus in the face and turned to Dean Blane. She shook her head. "There's no one else. Don't worry, it'll be a quick trip. You'll be back before classes on Monday."

"How? The train ride there and back takes most of a day."

"You'll only be taking the train as far as Central. From there you'll go the rest of the way by dark portal. We receive regular deliveries so it won't seem strange for the train to come and go an extra time today."

"Well, maybe I can arrange to have an engine delivered while I'm out. That way the day won't be a total loss."

"I got word you were trying to find one. What's that about?"

Conryu explained and when he finished she grinned. "That's about the most impractical thing I've ever heard of. Technically it violates the no technology rule, but I'll grant you an exemption since you're conducting a magical experiment. It'll be interesting to see if you can make it work. More importantly, it makes a perfect cover for your outing. Let's go, time's a-wasting."

"I can't just disappear without telling Maria and the club, they're all expecting me."

"I'll tell everyone what they need to know." Dean Blane stood up. They were almost pressed together in the small space. "All you need to focus on is your mission. I'll walk you to the train."

"Good luck, my boy." Angus was positively beaming at him.

At least someone was excited. Regardless of his wishes to the contrary, it seemed he was getting drawn deeper and deeper into the magical world. Mr. Kane had told him last summer the government regarded him as a valuable resource. They certainly weren't shy about using him. At least it was to help his home town. If they'd asked him to go to North Port or Santa Angeles on the west coast he might have complained more. Not that it would have probably done much good.

He followed Dean Blane out of Angus's office and down the hall. "Don't say anything about the mission outside of a warded room. There's no way to know who might be listening. I've assured our privacy in case you have any more questions. Listen to Terra and don't do anything they don't ask you to do."

"Don't worry about that. The last thing I want is to do more than necessary. Do you have any idea how long I'm going to be on call?"

"You're, what, eighteen? Given an average life span—"

"Okay, okay, I get it."

He followed Dean Blane down some back halls he didn't even know existed until they emerged from a small side door. She whispered something and a chill settled over him. The next thing he knew they were flying.

"Jesus!"

They went just high enough to clear the trees before landing on the train platform. Today only the engine and a single car waited on the tracks. The door was open and inside were piles of crates, sacks, and a bunch of shelves.

"Looks comfy."

"It's only half an hour. This train doesn't go to the station, but a warehouse. A Department car will meet you there. Good luck."

He stepped into the train and before he knew it they were moving.

* * *

Maria paced just inside the main doors of the lecture hall. Everyone else was busy with their clubs or studying so she had the large foyer to herself. Conryu was late again. That was getting to be a habit. She hoped the professor wasn't telling him more of his life's story. Conryu was one of the more patient and gentle people she knew, but even he had his breaking point.

Speaking of breaking points Maria was approaching her own with Mrs. Alustrial. Her light magic teacher wouldn't look at her much less acknowledge her questions in class. If there was a point she didn't understand she was out of luck. It didn't seem like a very professional attitude, but when ego was involved sometimes nothing else mattered.

"Maria." Dean Blane approached at a quick walk.

A queasy feeling settled in Maria's stomach. "Have you seen Conryu?"

"As a matter of fact I have."

"Oh?" Please let him be okay.

The dean muttered a spell. "He had to return to the city. An emergency came up and your father needed him for another breaking."

"Oh god. Is it something dangerous?"

"Not at all. It's just the magic involved is a little more than the wizards at the Department can handle. Don't worry, he'll be back by Monday."

She forced herself to take slow breaths. Dad wouldn't put Conryu in danger. "Thanks for telling me. I should probably get to my alchemy club."

"Actually." Dean Blane moved to block her when she took a step. "There's something I need you to do for me. While Conryu's task isn't dangerous, it is something we want kept quiet. I need you to take a message to the girls in his club. If I do it they might grow suspicious."

"Of course." If they were asking for favors this might be a good chance to get Mrs. Alustrial to straighten up her act. Maria hated dragging someone else into her problems, but there was nothing she could do on her own. "Maybe you could help me with something as well."

"Like what?"

Maria told her what was happening in her class. "I was hoping I could switch teachers."

Dean Blane frowned. "All the other light magic teachers have other classes. I'll have a talk with Mrs. Alustrial. I assure you when Monday rolls around, you'll have no further problems from her."

Maria shivered at the dean's cold tone. She wouldn't want to be on the receiving end of a lecture from the dean, not when she was in that mood. "So what did you want me to tell Conryu's club?"

"Tell them he's gone to Central to arrange an engine and that he won't be back until late." She gave Maria directions to the club's shed and they parted ways.

She left the lecture hall and trudged across the campus to the ragged little shack sitting right at the edge of the woods. Steam rose from the roof and all the snow was melted in a ten-yard circle around it. The promise of heat quickened her pace.

Maria knocked on the door and it slid open revealing Sonja and Crystal.

"Conryu?" Sonja sounded far too eager. "Oh, Maria right? He's not here."

"I know. Conryu asked me to bring you a message. Dean Blane gave him permission to go to Central to pick up an engine for your project. She's suspending the rules and calling it a magical experiment."

Sonja grinned. "It's about time. I was starting to wonder if this job was ever going to begin. How come he didn't tell us himself?"

Maria's heart raced. She hated lying. "It was a spur of the moment thing and he had to rush to catch the train. He won't be back until late tonight."

"Huh." Sonja looked up at Crystal. "Guess there's nothing to do today. Want to go to the cafeteria and have an ice cream?"

"Sure."

Sonja returned her attention to Maria. "You can join us if you'd like."

"No, thank you. I have to get to alchemy club." She fled before she had to answer any more questions.

* * *

It seemed like they'd barely gotten moving when the train began to slow down again. Conryu held on to the shelves until the final lurch. The door slid open at once and a middle-aged woman in a gray robe glared up at him.

"Well, come on then."

She moved to one side and he hopped down. Ten yards from the track was the biggest warehouse he'd ever seen. The black sedan parked next to it looked like a toy. The Department of Magic's pentagram logo was painted on the side of both car and warehouse.

The wizard marched toward it and he fell in step behind her. Not much for chit chat, these Department wizards. This one was every bit as friendly as the one that tested him.

She pointed at the back seat door and climbed in behind the wheel. He hadn't even gotten his seatbelt fastened when she stomped on the accelerator and they went screeching out of the lot. The buckle finally clicked into place and not a minute too soon the way his chauffeur drove. At least the soft leather of the seat was more comfortable than the sack of onions he sat on during the train ride.

"So is it safe to talk in here?" Conryu asked.

"Yep." She swerved around a dump truck, zipped past it, and pulled back in front.

"Do you know any more about what's happening?"

"Nope." She stepped harder on the gas.

Conryu caught a glimpse of the speedometer as it crept past eighty. "Did you by any chance ever drive a race car?"

That drew a laugh. "Boss wants you at HQ double quick. When the boss says jump you by god better jump."

"Who's the boss?"

She looked at him in the rearview mirror. "You kidding?"

"No, ma'am. Everything in this business is new to me. I assume you're talking about the Central Station Chief."

"Not just the Central Chief, Malice Kincade is the head of the whole Department. She answers only to the president, and some say he answers to her, at least on magical matters."

"Kincade, you mean the famous Kincades?"

"If it has to do with magic they're the only Kincades. Malice turned the business over to her middle daughter ten years ago when she took over the Department. I'm not the least ashamed to admit she scares the shit out of me."

The Department wizard fell silent after that. Conryu looked out the window at the Central City skyline. The various designs looked even more impressive up close. One in particular drew his eye, a black, cylindrical skyscraper maybe forty stories high. A ten-story pentagram was engraved in the glass. Talk about an intimidating building.

Ten minutes later they were parking in a connected garage. Conryu scrambled out, relieved to have made it in one piece, and followed his guide through a set of automatic double doors. Inside, the halls were gray and undecorated. Not so much as a single piece of art cluttered the walls. They stopped in front of a bank of elevators and she pressed the call button.

"So what's with the book?"

Conryu glanced down at Prime. "It has some notes Dean Blane thought might be useful."

The scholomantic sent its annoyance through their link, but the wizard appeared to accept his explanation. The elevator chimed and the doors slid open. She motioned Conryu in first then followed.

The control panel had four basement levels and thirty-eight above-ground levels. The Department wizard waved her hand in front of the panel and spoke a short phrase. It wasn't Infernal so he didn't know what she said. A basement level five button appeared and she pushed it.

She caught him staring and grinned. "We don't want just anyone to have access to the portal chambers."

The ride down took less than a minute. The doors opened on a long corridor. She motioned him out. "Just follow the hall to the central chamber then go through the black door. The boss is waiting for you."

Conryu stepped out and the door shut behind him. He blew out a sigh and started down the empty hall. Stupid wizards and their creepy hangouts. It felt like at least a hundred yards before the hall opened into a round chamber with six doors, one for each element.

The black door wasn't even like a painted black, it was more like the absence of all light and Conryu found he didn't want to touch it.

"Don't be such a coward," Prime muttered around his arm.

"Be quiet. No one's supposed to know about you."

The door didn't have a handle so Conryu reached out to give it a shove. When his fingers were six inches away a burst of dark energy leapt from his hand to the door. It didn't so much swing open as fade away.

Inside was an almost empty room with a circle carved into the stone floor nearly identical to the one from his awakening. Standing beside it was a woman in gray robes, her white hair pulled up into a severe bun. She held her hands clasped behind her back and stared at him with green eyes as hard as gems. Her wrinkles weren't quite as deep as Mrs. Umbra's, but it was a near thing.

"Conryu Koda."

He nodded and stepped into the room. His instincts said not to show this one any fear. If she caught so much as a hint of weakness he was doomed. "Malice Kincade, nice to meet you. Your granddaughter's in my class."

"I know. I know everything about you. I haven't decided whether you're the greatest threat this world has ever known, its best hope for the future, or both."

Conryu cocked his head. "Why would I be either? I have no ambitions beyond a hope, a vain one it seems, to live a quiet life. As long as the world leaves me alone, I'm content to return the favor."

"A man without ambition, how unusual. Perhaps you'll grow into it or maybe you'll be manipulated into serving the ambitions of others. Whatever the case, know this: if you become a threat I'll see you dead."

"Great. Maybe next time you people need some breaking done you should call someone else. You think I can't find a better way to spend my Sunday? And by the way, you should be nicer to Kelsie. She's a sweetheart and you and her mother both seem to stress her out. She's doing her best."

"Her best isn't good enough. She's a Kincade."

Conryu waited for more, but Malice seemed to consider that all the explanation required and in her mind maybe it was.

"In any case," Malice continued, "it's no concern of yours."

"You're wrong. Kelsie's my friend and I don't wish to see her in pain."

Malice glared at him and he glared right back. Conryu refused to let the vicious old woman intimidate him.

She finally looked away and moved closer to the circle. "Enough of this useless banter. You have a task to perform. The circle will carry you to the border of Hell. Call Cerberus and ride him to the end of the path. You'll emerge in the Sentinel City Department's portal chamber."

Conryu held up his forearm. "What's to stop Lucifer and the Dark Lady from interfering?"

"The path is warded against demons. Cerberus will only be able to enter because of your connection. Now go."

Conryu stepped into the circle. Malice took a clear crystal key on a thong out from around her neck and touched the edge of the circle.

Everything went black. He blinked and once again found himself a step from Hell.

* * *

Conryu looked around at vast amounts of nothing and sighed. It would be okay with him if he never had to come back here.

"Cerberus."

A pool of darkness gathered beside him and in moments the demon dog formed a body half again as big as a horse. All three heads panted, their tongues hanging out. The center head leaned down and licked him.

"Good to see you too. Crouch down so I can climb on, please." Cerberus lay down on his belly and Conryu leapt up onto his broad back. "We'd best be on our way before any unwelcome guests arrive."

Cerberus whined and his body trembled under Conryu.

"What is it?"

"Back again, mortal?" a familiar, deep voice said. Lucifer emerged from the endless darkness, the demon shining with his own inner light. He held the massive trident over one shoulder like Paul Bunyan with his ax.

Conryu didn't want to get into a discussion with the demon. "I'm just passing through. Come on, Cerberus."

The demon dog set out at a trot that soon accelerated into a full run. Lucifer kept pace easily. "No need to rush off, boy."

Conryu ignored him, drawing a rumbling growl from Lucifer. The trident rose and plunged down at them.

Conryu flinched, but it struck an invisible barrier a foot above his head. He blew out a sigh. Malice hadn't lied about the ward anyway.

Lucifer hammered the barrier several more times with equally futile results. "The Department of Magic's wards are as impressive as always. Wouldn't you prefer make a contract with me rather than that puppy?"

Cerberus's left-hand head growled, but Lucifer ignored it. Conryu ignored the demon's looming presence. It felt like they were covering vast distances with each stride. Hopefully they would reach the exit soon.

"Come now, be reasonable. If I were to contract with you I could lend you a portion of my power. Strong as you are now, teamed with me you'd be invincible. You can't ask for more than that."

Conryu finally looked at Lucifer. "Until you decide to betray me? I've been warned about your nature. You weren't christened the Prince of Lies for nothing. I don't trust you and I can't very well team up with someone I don't trust. Cerberus has proven himself a loyal partner and that's worth more than raw power."

Up ahead a light appeared. That had to be the exit gate.

"Deny me, boy, and Hell will never be a safe place for you. Every time you enter I'll be waiting. One of these days you'll make a mistake and when you do I'll rip the screaming soul from your body and drag it down to the darkest pit I can find." With that final threat Lucifer vanished.

Cerberus's right head looked back at him and whined.

"Yeah, he's a real charmer. Don't worry, we'll be extra careful." Cerberus came to a stop six feet from the disk of light and lay down to let Conryu climb off his back. He patted the demon dog on his flank. "Thanks for the ride."

Conryu stepped into the light and left Hell behind.

* * *

Lady Raven reclined on the soft velvet of her couch and sighed. In the five months since she'd been forced to abandon two of her identities she'd turned her lair... She smiled to herself. Calling the place a lair made her sound like a witch in a storybook. Hideout perhaps? No, that carried a sort of gangster feel. Redoubt perhaps, that had a properly secure sound to it.

She turned her head to regard Iron Skull's reanimated body. It stood silently against the stone wall. "What do you think? Shall we call this our redoubt?"

Of course the Faceless One occupying the body was incapable of responding. It simply stared straight ahead with its empty black gaze. Though powerful and obedient, her new servants weren't much for company. Six more months and she could leave her dingy temporary home for a place befitting a newly risen Hierarch.

She'd sensed it when the weakling Department wizards approached her hidden boxes along with their feeble attempts to dispel her wards. They were both pathetic, but she gave them credit for at least hunting the boxes down. She'd harbored doubts that they were capable of that much. Terra and Clair had even been kind enough to add an extra layer of protection to her hiding places.

How frustrating it must be for the Department to know the locations and still be totally powerless to do anything. She almost laughed aloud, but instead sighed. She should summon a familiar to share her victory with. It was terribly unsatisfying having no one but undead to whom she could gloat.

The familiar tug from her mask drew Lady Raven's attention to the end table in the corner of her lounge. It wasn't time for the monthly report, she'd just spoken to her superiors last week. She rolled off her couch, walked over, and grabbed the mask. What did they want?

A door in the left-hand wall led to her new casting chamber. She entered and sealed it behind her. When she reached the casting circle in the center of the room she cleared her mind and slipped the mask on.

Lady Raven was instantly taken to the meeting place where she found only Lady Wolf waiting. She'd never been summoned by less than the full group. "Hierarch?"

"Your hiding places are compromised. The boxes must be moved at once."

"As I said last week, the Department wizards are powerless to damage my wards. I assure you the artifacts are in no danger."

"They've summoned the abomination. Are you so confident your defenses will hold against his power?"

Lady Raven swallowed. If the boy was coming he'd destroy her wards in a second. "I'll move them at once. May I ask how you learned of his arrival?"

"Our agent in Central alerted us. He's traveling by dark portal if he isn't there already. Your time is short, Lady Raven. Do not fail us."

Lady Wolf vanished and she was alone in her casting chamber. Conryu Koda again. The boy wizard was turning into the bane of her existence. Fortunately she'd made arrangements for just such an emergency. Five months was a long time to prepare and she hadn't spent all her time on interior decorating.

When he arrived at the first location she'd have a surprise waiting for him and his friends.

* * *

Conryu stepped out of the light, leaving Lucifer and Cerberus behind. When his vision cleared he found himself in a chamber very similar to the one in Central. The black disk he was standing on had the exact same rune pattern.

"Conryu! This way."

He spun and found Mr. Kane waving to him from beside the room's only door. Terra and Lin were with him. Conryu jogged over. The moment he cleared the dark circle the power vanished. Though he knew Lucifer couldn't break through the wards he felt a good deal better now that the portal had closed.

He reached Mr. Kane and the little group hustled through the door. "I trust your trip went smoothly."

"I'm not sure smoothly is the word I'd use, but I made it." Conryu followed Mr. Kane to the nearby elevators with Lin and Terra bringing up the rear. "So you need me to break some more wards?"

"Yes. The team finally tracked down all five boxes, but we can't access them."

"How strong are the wards?" Conryu asked as they rode the elevator upstairs.

"I estimate twice as strong as the one you broke for us last time," Terra said.

Conryu nodded. That shouldn't cause him any problems.

Prime wriggled free of his grasp and flew up to look Terra in the eye. "What did you do with the necroplasma?"

"It's still in my casting chamber trapped in the spell circle. I'll figure out how best to deal with it once we've collected Mercia's gifts."

The doors opened and they stepped out into the lobby. "I'll leave you with Lin and Terra. Thanks again for your help, Conryu." Mr. Kane started back into the elevator.

"Will I have a chance to visit my parents?"

"I don't think so. We need to get you back to school ASAP. Dean Blane called me after you left. I've made arrangements for an engine to be sent to the academy."

Conryu frowned at that. He'd planned to choose the motor himself and he needed his tools. Terra grabbed his sleeve and pulled him toward the exit, not giving him a chance to complain. "We don't have time to waste on idle chatter. The longer those boxes remain in place the more opportunity for something to go wrong."

Mr. Kane waved as he was dragged away. Conryu freed himself from Terra's grasp and followed her and Lin in a more dignified posture. They stepped out into the bright morning sun.

A tan four-door Department sedan idled by the curb. Lin slipped behind the wheel and Terra sat beside him leaving Conryu stuck in the back seat. At least with Lin driving Conryu didn't fear for his life.

They pulled out and headed east toward the docks. Conryu stared out the window. It was good to be home, even if only for a day.

"I never understood you humans' fondness for your home towns." Prime settled on the seat beside him. "It's not like demons pine for home every time some wizard summons us."

"You live in Hell. Who'd be eager to return there?"

"Good point. Lucifer certainly didn't seem pleased to see you again."

"No kidding. We have to figure out how to remove his name from my arm, the Dark Lady's too. Not that I wouldn't mind seeing her again."

"Did she leave a lingering enchantment on you?" Prime flew up and looked him all over.

Conryu was pretty sure the only enchantment she left was in his overactive imagination.

Terra looked back at him. "What's this about seeing Lucifer?"

"He tried to kill me again on my way here, but the wards held. I was just saying I need to get his brand off my arm so he won't be able to tell the moment I enter a portal."

"I noticed some fluctuations in the magic while we were waiting for you. That must have been what I detected. You seem rather calm considering you were almost killed by the devil."

"Yeah, well, I wasn't anywhere near this calm the first time. So do you want me to do a proper breaking or just use Dispel?"

"Dispel," Terra answered at once. "I want every bit of magic in the vicinity wiped out."

"I chanted the spell five times before releasing it once and negated every spell within sixty yards. Will that be enough?"

She stared at him for a moment. "That should do it." She turned back around, muttering, but he couldn't make out what she said.

Half an hour later Lin pulled in beside a chain link fence with a door in it. Beyond the fence was a flat expanse of concrete with a gully running through it. Conryu said, "Reveal." The culvert at the end of the gully lit up. Maybe that was the wrong way to describe the inky black lines running everywhere, but that was how he thought of it.

"I take it the box is down there."

"Yes. Mercia left it on a living pedestal along with a bunch of zombies to guard it." Terra opened her door and climbed out. Conryu and Lin joined her with Prime bringing up the rear.

"Speaking of the zombies," Lin said. "I spoke to my contacts at the morgue. They were all killed by a single stab wound to the chest. Missing persons is trying to match them to any outstanding cases."

"They must have been Mercia's sacrifices." Terra shook her head and led the way over to the culvert.

They stopped well back and Conryu eyed the dark opening. It certainly looked like a place you'd hide a dark magic artifact. "Shall I get on with it?"

"Please. Hurl your spell as deep into the culvert as you can. Don't hold back as we may not have a second chance."

Don't hold back. There was something he didn't hear very often. Conryu crossed his wrists and fingers and began the chant. When he hit five repetitions and the dark sphere was as big as a pumpkin he hurled it at the opening.

Seconds later a wash of dark magic shot out of the culvert, dissipating five feet from them. The wards were gone and he was about to ask where they were headed next when a flash of power burst from the opening.

Shrill screams came from the culvert followed a moment later by a pair of black-winged demons just like the ones that had tried to attack him last summer. The demons flew into the air and spat dark energy at Terra.

She hurled flames and the two energies negated each other. Conryu cast, "Cloak of Darkness!" and dark magic covered both himself and Prime.

Lin drew his pistol and put half a clip into the rightmost demon. If the creature felt the bullets it gave no sign, though it did turn to look at Lin. It opened its fang-filled mouth.

Conryu crossed his fingers and raised a hand. The moment dark energy shot from the demon's mouth he shouted, "Break!"

A sphere of dark energy streaked from his hand and negated the blast.

"Thanks." Lin put his gun away and turned towards Conryu. "What can I do?"

"Not a thing," Prime said. "Only magic can hurt demons."

Lin looked hopefully at Conryu. "Sorry, Sarge, they don't teach offensive spells to first-year students."

Terra was busy exchanging blasts with the first demon leaving the second to focus on him and Lin. Conryu negated another attack. At least the demon hadn't gotten it in its head to fly down and tear them apart.

"Prime, how do we stop them?"

"You could banish them. I have the spell here." Prime started to flip to the proper page.

The spell Mrs. Umbra had used took half a minute to cast and he hadn't even recognized a quarter of the words she used. No way could he memorize and cast such a complex spell under these circumstances.

"That's no good. All I really need is to make them stop attacking."

They ran from another blast. The concrete steamed where the dark energy touched it.

"Try commanding them," Prime said. "A powerful dark wizard can sometimes dominate a demon if they focus all their will on it."

"Your will makes the magic happen, not the words or gestures," Conryu muttered.

That's what Mrs. Umbra had said. It was time to test that theory.

He focused his mind on the demons and having them cease attacking. "Stop!" he shouted in Infernal.

Both demons shuddered and twitched, but their mouths shut and they stopped breathing those dark blasts. Terra ran over to join them.

"Don't break your concentration. I'll open a portal then you order them through."

Terra moved a little ways away and chanted an unfamiliar spell. A black ring appeared and slowly filled in until it became a disk. The demons saw it and struggled harder.

Conryu grit his teeth. "Be still!"

The demons quieted again.

"Okay, Conryu. Order them through."

He pictured the demons flying through the portal. "Go to Hell!"

The demons plunged down out of the sky and vanished through the portal. The instant they vanished Terra spoke a word and the gate closed.

Conryu fell to his knees, the mother of all headaches pounding behind his eyes.

* * *

Terra stared for a moment as Conryu knelt and grasped his head. She knew enough about the academy curriculum to know they didn't teach freshmen how to control demons. In fact she was fairly certain that was a third-year subject. He'd done it with nothing but sheer force of will and raw magical power. Absolutely stunning.

Unfortunately for him, Conryu was now paying the price. Wizards used spells for a reason and one of them was to avoid a backlash from channeling too much unrefined energy. The fact that he used chaotic dark magic made it even worse. On the plus side they were all still alive because of him. If he hadn't been here Terra doubted she'd have defeated both demons on her own.

"You okay?"

Conryu looked at her with bloodshot eyes. "Sure. You don't have any aspirin, do you? I have a horrible headache."

"Sorry. If it's any consolation it wouldn't have helped anyway. Your headache is from magical backlash. Only time or proper application of light magic will make it go away."

"I don't suppose you know how to apply it?"

"Nope. All I know are the basics of light magic." Terra shook her head. "We should have brought Shizuku. She'd have you fixed up in a blink."

"I'll survive either way. If you don't need me I'm going to sit in the car."

"No problem. I'll collect the box and we'll get out of here."

She headed for the culvert and Lin took a step to follow. Terra shook her head and mouthed, "Stay with him."

He turned back to help Conryu to his feet. The two of them started for the car and Terra put them out of her mind. Her spell didn't reveal any lingering magic, but that didn't mean she was in the clear. The moment she let her guard down was the moment she might die.

At the mouth of the culvert she conjured a trio of flame orbs. She sent one to fly ahead of her and kept the others by her side. The walk to the rear of the culvert took only seconds. Where the fleshy mound had once sat there was nothing but a rotten, misshapen heap of stinking gobbets of flesh. Terra devoutly hoped the box wasn't buried in the mess.

She narrowed her eyes and looked closer. There wasn't so much as a hint of magic to be found. As powerful as Conryu's spell was it should still have spared the contents of the box. If she couldn't detect anything...

"No, no, no. Scream, winds from beyond, Gale Gust!" She conjured a focused blast of wind that sent gobbets of flesh flying everywhere. No box. "Damn it!"

Somehow Mercia had moved it to a new hiding place. That begged the question of how she managed it and more to the point, how did she know she needed to.

Terra left the culvert and stalked over to the car. Conryu was lying down in the back, his arm over his eyes.

"Where is it?" Lin asked.

"Gone."

"Gone? Where?"

"Damned if I know. Let's head to the next location. I need to check something." She craned her neck to look in the back seat. "How you holding up?"

75

Conryu lowered his arm. "I'm better, thanks. So did I half melt my brain for nothing?"

"I wouldn't say for nothing. We would have had to deal with that trap at some point, but we didn't recover the box. It's been relocated. For the life of me I can't figure how she did it."

"Maybe she moved it through a dark portal. Mrs. Umbra's had me and Prime working on that so if we're separated I can call him to my side."

Terra nodded. "Maybe. The problem is the clues that led us to these hiding places made no mention of backups. I suspect Mercia didn't tell her thugs. Wise move on her part."

Conryu sat up, groaned, and lay back down. "So what now? You need me to clear those other locations?"

"Afraid so, but first I'm going to look and see if the box is still there and your Dispel triggered its disappearance or if it's already gone. We might be able to work around the former, but if it's the latter we're screwed."

* * *

Conryu shuffled through the doors and down to the elevators. Midnight had come and gone and they'd finally made it back to the Department of Magic. He'd dispelled all the wards and traps, helped banish five more demons, and convinced Lin and Terra to buy him three slices of Giovanni's pizza. That had easily been the highlight of the trip.

Though Terra insisted the work he'd done was important and he might even believe it after ten hours' sleep, right now it felt like he wasted the day. The whole point of this mission was to recover those stupid boxes and there'd been no sign of them. No one would even tell him why they were so important.

Worse, at least for Conryu, if Terra and Lin somehow found them again he'd probably have to come back to repeat the process.

"Jesus, Conryu, you look horrible."

He glanced up to find Mr. Kane standing beside the elevator. He had a key that appeared to be made out of crystal and the mate to Malice's.

"It's been a long day. If I never see another flying demon it'll be too soon."

Mr. Kane looked to Terra. "Boxes?"

"No sign of them, Chief. Mercia must have known we were coming and relocated them."

Mr. Kane pressed his palms to his forehead and Conryu wasn't sure if he wanted to scream or cry. "So we're back to square one."

"Actually we're in worse shape than before as we now have no clue where to resume our search." Everyone turned to glare at Lin which made Conryu smile. It was always a nice feeling not to be the one in trouble.

"I'm sure you guys will sort it all out. I either need to get back or find somewhere to sleep." Conryu yawned for emphasis.

"Right." Mr. Kane pressed the call button. "You have classes tomorrow."

"Today. In about seven hours as a matter of fact. I may take a sick day."

"Don't do that." Mr. Kane stepped into the elevator and Conryu followed. They started down to the basement. "Anything out of the ordinary may attract unwanted attention."

"Me falling asleep in class would be out of the ordinary and if I had to cast a spell I might faint. I'll just put it down to food poisoning or something."

They left the elevator and entered the portal chamber. Mr. Kane touched the edge of the circle with the crystal key and it turned black. "Do what you think best. And thanks again for your help."

Conryu took a step toward the portal then turned back. "Be sure they send a full set of tools with the engine. I'm going to have to tear it all the way down."

Mr. Kane gave him a thumbs up and he stepped into the portal.

Chapter 5

Back at School

Conryu staggered into his room around four in the morning. He couldn't even remember the ride through Hell beyond Cerberus's worried whining. Kelsie's grandmother may have made some vague threat, but he was so tired he just ignored her. The train wasn't ready when he arrived so he ended up sitting around by the warehouse for three hours. All in all he'd had better days.

"At least you survived." Prime flew over to his desk and settled in his usual spot.

Considering how much he felt like a zombie, he wasn't sure he had survived. He collapsed on the bed, not even bothering to undress. Some time later he was vaguely aware of Prime snarling at the pixie that came to fetch him to class until she fled. Conryu sent mental gratitude to the scholomantic and fell back asleep.

When he woke up again it was an empty stomach that did it. He had no idea what time it was, though well after lunch seemed a fair guess. Conryu rolled out of bed, staggered into the bathroom and let the naiad wash his hair and back.

Clean clothes combined with the shower had him feeling almost human again. The next order of business was hunting up something to eat. The thought had barely crossed his mind when someone knocked.

When he opened the door he couldn't say what pleased him more, seeing Maria waiting outside or the overstuffed sandwich she had in her hands. "Please say that's for me."

"It's for you. When you missed lunch I figured you'd be hungry." Maria brushed past him and into his room. She looked around and shook her head. "What a mess."

"Give me a break. I had a busy day yesterday."

"Yeah, Dean Blane gave me the short version. How'd it go?"

"Not as well as they hoped. You know I can't say much here, right?"

She nodded and handed him the sandwich, ham and cheese with extra mustard, just the way he liked it. Conryu took a bite and sighed. "Have I told you lately that I love you?"

"It's been a few days, but I'll forgive you. The girls in your club were excited when I told them you'd gone to arrange an engine. You didn't forget, did you?"

"Nope. Should be here by the end of the week."

"Are you really going to try and make it run on nothing but magic?"

"Sure, why not?" He polished off the sandwich and found himself looking for a drink.

"Do you want all the reasons why not, or just the obvious ones?"

"I don't actually want any of them. I was just looking for a project to cheer Sonja up. Though the idea of a motorcycle with a magic engine sounds way cool."

Maria wiped a spot of mustard off his face. "Well it took you half the year, but you managed to incorporate mechanic work into your studies. I figured it would take longer."

He grinned. "What time is it?"

"Around three. You slept through all your classes."

He shrugged. "Other than the one with Mrs. Umbra I could take or leave the rest."

"Not if you want to graduate."

She had him there.

* * *

Twenty minutes after Maria left a pixie arrived with a rolled-up message. He read it while she waited. It was short and to the point. "My office, now." Signed Mrs. Umbra. Conryu handed the note back to the pixie, grabbed Prime, and waved her out. "After you."

He followed the tiny elemental out of the dorm, across the snow-covered field to the main hall. Once they were inside he was surprised to head upstairs instead of to the basement. He'd assumed the head of dark magic would have her office downstairs.

They left the classrooms and continued on past the administrative offices. Several secretaries stared at him as he passed by, but since he had the pixie guiding him they must have assumed he had permission to be there. After what felt like a half-mile hike they stopped in front of a black, rune-covered door. That was more like it. He almost didn't want to knock.

Luck was on his side and the door opened before he had to touch it. Beyond the door was a small office with a desk, chairs, and book-stuffed shelves. He restrained a sigh. Every time he expected to end up somewhere ominous it ended up being normal. All the weird shit seemed to happen when he least expected it.

Mrs. Umbra sat behind her desk. She waved him over to one of the empty chairs and when he'd sat she said, "I heard all about it. How's your head?"

"Fine. I slept off the worst of the backlash. I don't remember it hurting that much when I summoned Cerberus."

"You were barely conscious that time. It's way worse when you're aware of what's happening."

"No kidding, but I survived, that's what counts."

"How did you manage the other five demons without losing consciousness?"

"Please don't get mad."

The wrinkles in her forehead deepened. "Conryu?"

"I had Prime teach me the domination spell." He winced, but she didn't blast him where he sat. "I know I'm not supposed to study anything without your permission, but it was an emergency."

"Did it give you any trouble?"

"Not really. It was longer than the spells I've cast so far, but the increased power didn't bother me. I had a little trouble with this twisty, flip thing you have to do with your off hand halfway through, but I figured it out after a couple practice runs. I'll be honest, it doesn't seem hard enough to be a third-year spell."

She shook her head. "That's because you're so much stronger than average. Domination requires you to channel ten times as much energy as Cloak of Darkness, for example. The spells aren't the problem. The reason it's a third-year spell is because it takes two years to build up enough capability with dark energy for most wizards to cast it and remain conscious."

"Oh. I have to say it was way easier than using willpower to control the demons. Once I hit them with it they went as docile as kittens. I wish I'd known it to begin with. Would have saved me one hell of a headache."

Mrs. Umbra groaned, opened her mouth like she was going to say something, then closed it again. After a moment she said, "I hear you met Malice Kincade."

"Don't get me started on her. Why is it that so many people feel the need to include a threat when they first speak to me? And I told her she should be nicer to Kelsie."

Mrs. Umbra laughed and leaned back in her chair. When she'd wiped a tear from her eye she asked, "How'd she take it?"

"Not seriously. I don't think I convinced her, but I still had to say something."

"Don't worry about it. You understand you can't talk to anyone about what happened yesterday, right?"

"Yeah, not that I really know all that much. Demons being summoned inside the city doesn't seem like the sort of thing the Department would want getting around. I hate not being able to tell Maria though. It feels like I'm lying to her."

"I'm familiar with that experience. If it's any consolation it's not your fault you can't tell her."

"It's not, but thanks."

Conryu's chat with Mrs. Umbra ended with her promising to teach him more advanced spells in such a tone that he broke out into a sweat. He went back to the dorm ready for another nap. At the bottom of the steps he found Kelsie standing outside his room.

"Hey."

She jumped and spun to face him. "I thought you were inside."

"No, Mrs. Umbra wanted to talk with me. How are you?"

"Worried about you. When you didn't come to class this morning I figured you must have been sick." She was kneading her hands and fidgeting.

She really did seem concerned. He felt a little bad about worrying her, not that he'd had much choice. "It was a stomach bug, something I ate didn't agree with me. I'm fine now. Would you like to come in?"

He opened the door and she ducked inside. Kelsie sat on the edge of the bed. Conryu put Prime on the desk and plopped down in his chair. "So what did I miss?"

"Not much. We practiced circle casting the whole time. Mrs. Lenore was going to start our fusion magic lessons, but she said tomorrow would be fine."

"Since I wasn't there. Sorry."

"No, no, it's okay. I'm just excited to give it a try. What did Mrs. Umbra want?"

"Just to discuss what we are going to work on for the rest of the year. Boring stuff, really." Yet another lie, but he didn't have any choice.

* * *

Kelsie's hands trembled as she walked down the steps to dark magic. She'd gotten pretty good at working with her partner in the casting circle. Between them they'd managed to dispel the light, but not shatter the sphere. It was a beginning at least. Today she was supposed to start fusion training with Conryu. He was so strong the idea terrified her. Why did she even agree to work with him?

Because he was her friend, maybe the only one she'd ever had. The evening before, when he'd invited her into his room, for a moment she'd feared her mother had been right and he was going to try something, but he couldn't have been more polite.

She blew out a sigh and reached for the classroom door. Part of her was annoyed that he didn't try anything and another part knew she'd be furious if he did. What a screwed up way of thinking.

Kelsie stepped inside and found she was the last one to arrive, even the perpetually late Mrs. Lenore had arrived ahead of her. Her cheeks burned when everyone turned to look at her. Conryu just grinned and pulled out the chair beside him for her. She rushed to sit down.

"Okay, now that we're all here," Mrs. Lenore said. "We're going to try something different. Some of you, I've noticed, seem to have the two-person circle casting down, so you'll be trying three-person circles. Meg, you and Caitlin will continue as a pair. Conryu and Kelsie will try fusion casting."

Mrs. Lenore set about instructing the girls on a three-person circle. Kelsie tried to pay attention since she'd have to do it at some point as well, but she couldn't get her mind off Conryu. He sat beside her with the most indifferent expression. He clearly couldn't have cared less about circle casting. For him it must be like a tiger listening to a bunch of house cats receive instructions on hunting mice.

Once the circles were going Mrs. Lenore motioned them over to the corner of the classroom. She set one of the glowing spheres on an empty table. "So the way this is supposed to work is, Kelsie, you stand behind Conryu and put your hand on the center of his back. When he casts the spell you'll feel like something is pulling at you. You just need to relax and let your power flow so it melds with his. If this works the way it's supposed to, you two should create a more powerful result than Conryu would on his own. Shall we give it a try?"

Kelsie moved to stand behind him. She tried to dry the sweat off her hand, but it only lasted for a second. She put her palm on Conryu's back.

He glanced over his shoulder. "Ready?"

"Yes." It came out as more of a squeak than a real affirmative.

"Here we go." He raised his hand. "Darkness bind..."

A thrum of power ran through her, shaking her to the bone. She could no longer make out what he was saying. The psychic vibrations increased with each word until he completed the spell. In her mind's eye a deep, black pit appeared and six glowing red eyes stared back at her.

The pulling Mrs. Lenore described felt more like her soul being wrenched from her body. The darkness inside him was trying to devour her.

Kelsie broke the connection and fled the room. She stumbled down the hall, her heart racing and her breath coming in gasps. A few feet from the door she fell to her knees and tried not to hyperventilate as tears poured from her eyes.

A hand on her back returned her to the moment. She looked up to find Mrs. Lenore staring at her.

"What happened, dear?"

Kelsie described the darkness and the eyes. "It was so overwhelming I panicked. I'm sorry."

"It's my fault. I didn't expect you to be able to see into his portal. Those eyes were Cerberus. Conryu was forced to make a pact with him to keep minor demons from slipping through the gate every time he casts a spell. You don't need to be afraid, the demon dog can't affect anything in our world."

"But it felt like he was trying to pull my soul out of my body."

"I didn't expect that either. Maybe I should have practiced this with Conryu myself before I tried to instruct you." Mrs. Lenore hung her head. "I'm a terrible teacher."

Now Kelsie felt equally bad about upsetting Mrs. Lenore and jealous at the idea of someone else practicing with Conryu.

She straightened and pulled Mrs. Lenore with her. "I'm okay now. I'd like to give it another try."

"Are you sure? I don't want to force you."

She nodded once. "I'm sure."

* * *

Conryu stared as Mrs. Lenore ran after Kelsie. He didn't know what had her so upset. Everything was going smoothly then bang, she broke contact and ran off. It screwed up the spell and now the glowing sphere sat on the table mocking him. While he had no doubt about his ability to destroy the thing on his own, that wasn't the point of the exercise.

The other girls had stopped their practice and were glaring at him. People seemed to enjoy glaring at him and he was getting sick of it. He hadn't done anything wrong. At least he didn't think he had.

Finally Kelsie and Mrs. Lenore returned. Kelsie's cheeks were red and she'd been crying. He still couldn't figure out what had bothered her.

She didn't say anything, simply moved around behind him and put her hand on his back. "Let's try again."

He looked at Mrs. Lenore who nodded.

Well, here goes. "Darkness bind our power as one, Break and Shatter!" He focused on the sphere and compelled the magic to affect nothing else. When he finished Kelsie stiffened, but didn't run.

A black lance of energy shot out and struck the sphere. One second it was there and the next not even a pile of metal shavings remained.

He grinned. That's the way it was supposed to work.

Kelsie took her hand off his back and peeked around him. "Where's the sphere?"

"Gone. We obliterated it. Good work, partner." He gave her hand a squeeze and she managed a weak smile.

"Let's call that good for today, you two," Mrs. Lenore said. "Kelsie, why don't you try working with Meg and Caitlin on a trio casting."

Kelsie looked up at him then nodded and went to join the other girls. When they were fully engrossed in their practice Mrs. Lenore said, "She caught a glimpse of Cerberus and it scared her."

Having seen Cerberus up close he understood how she might have that reaction. "What did you say to calm her down?"

"Beats me, I'm glad she pulled it together though. How did the spell feel?"

"I didn't notice much difference. I know I'm not supposed to ask, but what did she score on the test?"

"I guess it couldn't hurt to tell you, but keep it to yourself. She pulled a nine hundred, respectable but not above average."

"That's less than ten percent of my full power."

Mrs. Lenore nodded. "We're just going through the motions here, I recognize that, but I don't know what else to do."

Conryu didn't either. Maybe Mrs. Umbra would have some more ideas.

Class wrapped up and the girls all left. Ten minutes later Mrs. Umbra arrived. She had a scroll in her left hand, bigger than the one the pixie brought, but still not huge.

"Did you bring me a present?"

"No. This is a diagram of how a normal wizard develops." She spread it out on the big desk and when it tried to roll back up she muttered something that made it go rigid. "Now pay attention."

Conryu moved up beside her and examined the scroll. It didn't make for very exciting reading. There was a series of four bars, each more full than the last.

Mrs. Umbra pointed at the first one. "This represents a typical first-year student. She would be able to use about a third of her power safely by the end of the year. The percentage increases each year until the new wizard reaches her full potential in her final year. That is our most important task, shepherding young wizards through these critical first four years. We've chosen the spells and techniques we teach carefully so as not to overwhelm new wizards."

"What does that mean for me?"

"It means following our standard curriculum is pointless. I don't need to ease you through the process because, for some reason, you're already operating at full strength. If I taught you the most powerful spell I know you could cast it without batting an eye. There's one problem. Regardless of its pointlessness, we only have the one lesson plan and you'll graduate before the Department approves a new one."

Conryu's headache was coming back. "So, what, I just show up, put in my time, and pass whatever the final is?"

"Basically. Feel free to learn anything you like from your book, just don't cast any new spells without me. The only reason I restricted you was for your safety. Now that it's clear you're in no danger you may as well learn whatever you can."

An overwhelming urge to beat his head against the wall came over Conryu. Not only was he stuck learning a subject that didn't interest him, now his teacher tells him the whole process was pointless. If not for the law he'd be just as well off studying at home in his spare time and coming in to take the tests.

Four years of his life flushed down the toilet to no apparent purpose. Fantastic.

* * *

The rest of the week passed quickly. Conryu and Kelsie worked on fusion magic for ten minutes every day before she went to practice circle casting with the other girls, leaving him free to study his Infernal. There were still a lot of words he didn't know and until he was fluent in the language his dark magic potential remained limited.

90

Sunday arrived at last and with it his weekly visit with Angus. The boring visits used to annoy him, now he hoped the professor didn't have any news for him, especially today as he was supposed to meet the supply train and collect the engine and tools Mr. Kane had arranged for him. He was a little nervous, not knowing what style of motor he'd find. Hopefully it would be something simple, without a lot of computer-controlled components he'd have to work around.

Angus's door was open when he arrived which was a good sign. Conryu poked his head in and relaxed when he found the professor alone. "Please tell me you don't have any messages?"

"No, though I'm curious how you made out on your mission." Angus looked at him, all bright-eyed and eager.

"I'm not sure how much I'm allowed to say so you'd better ask Mr. Kane about it. See you next week."

Conryu left the crestfallen professor behind and jogged toward the train platform. Maria said she was working with her light magic teacher today so he didn't have to meet her until dinner. He didn't know what had happened last week, but Maria seemed more content than she had since winter break. She was also determined to be at the top of her class after finals.

He smiled. No one could fault Maria's dedication when it came to schoolwork. He hated it, but when a bunch of crazy wizards wanted you dead there wasn't much to be done. Not to mention it seemed he'd be on call to lend the Department a hand anytime they needed him.

That didn't seem right, but according to Mr. Kane he was the only one available powerful enough to do what was required, at least until the northern incursion was sorted out and god only knew how long that would be, summer at least. So for now he was their only option. With any luck it would be a temporary thing.

After a short, cold walk he arrived at the platform. His engine, a mercifully simple, single-cylinder job that looked like it came from a dirt bike, was sitting on a black pallet beside a large toolbox. Off to one side the delivery people unloaded boxes of food and other supplies. One of the teachers, a water wizard in her mid forties with a stern air about her, was overseeing the unloading, marking items off a list as they were brought out.

He was reluctant to bother her, but Conryu had no idea how he was supposed to transport the engine without a forklift or something.

Conryu bit the bullet and walked over to the teacher. "Excuse me?"

She looked at him wearing the same expression with which you might regard a puppy that shit on the rug. "I was told to expect you. You should know I don't approve of violating the no technology ban."

"Well, we're turning the engine into something that runs on magic, so that will make it a magic item when we're finished and that won't break any rules, right?"

She grunted.

"Anyway, how am I supposed to move it to our workshop?"

"No one explained to you how the lift pallets work?"

He wanted to tell her that if someone had explained to him how the pallets worked he wouldn't have asked her, but instead he just shook his head.

"Just touch the master rune, that's the biggest one on the pallet, and it will lift off the ground and follow you until you touch it again. Simple."

"Thank you, ma'am."

Conryu followed her instructions and was soon trudging toward the club's shack with the pallet following along behind like a dog at heel. A path had been cut through the snow, so it only took him a few minutes to make the walk.

When he arrived steam was rising off the roof and the door was cracked open, a warm glow leaking out. The moment he opened the door Sonja bounced to her feet and rushed over to the pallet. She pushed it in and touched the rune without so much as a hello.

Crystal was seated on the floor, still looking glum about not making the team, her hands held out toward the fire orb that was heating the place. She stood up with obvious reluctance and ambled over to the pallet which now rested on the ground.

"You got it, awesome." Sonja circled the engine, a huge smile on her face. She looked up at him. "What now?"

"Now I'll tear it apart, clean everything, and show you how it all works. Unless you guys are familiar with engines already."

Crystal shook her head. "All I know is that they start when I turn the key. You really think we can make this thing run on magic?"

"I don't see why not. One type of energy should motivate it as well as another."

"The only reason we might fail is a lack of imagination," Sonja said. "And that's one thing I have plenty of."

Conryu started working on the engine and by the time noon rolled around he had it mostly torn down. He explained what everything did as he went and by the time they parted ways the girls seemed confident they could have it going no problem.

Chapter 6

The Hunt for Mercia

Terra scratched the final rune in the side of her lantern. She'd been working on the artifact twelve hours a day every day for the past three weeks. At last the task was complete.

She tossed her tiny chisel onto her workshop table and wiped the sweat from her forehead. She called the device a lantern because it almost exactly resembled an old-fashioned metal-and-glass hurricane lamp. The difference was this one didn't give off light, instead it would hold the blob of necroplasma that bounced incessantly against the unseen walls of the spell circle that still held it.

With any luck her creation would act like a compass, leading them to Mercia. After their failure last month to secure the boxes they had no other hope than to locate Mercia and capture or kill her before she triggered the summoning. Failing that... Terra didn't want to think about it.

Taking up the device Terra went to the opposite side of the room and studied the erratic black blob as it struggled to escape its prison. You'd think the thing would wear out after a while, but so far it hadn't stopped moving since she captured it.

She set the lantern beside the spell circle and frowned. Though preparing the artifact had taken the most time, transferring the necroplasma was the most difficult part of the project. The fact that she was completely unfamiliar with the substance didn't make the task any easier.

Why hadn't she taken the time to consult with Conryu's scholomantic when it was here? She reluctantly admitted it was her overconfidence, thinking that they'd be able to retrieve the boxes and thus wouldn't have any need of the blob that had led to her mistake in judgment. Well, stuff happened, now she had to deal with it.

She removed the glass portion of the lantern revealing the rune-inscribed chamber that would hold the blob. A deep breath cleared her mind and she began a dark magic domination spell. It wasn't powerful enough to control a demon, but she should be able to use it to coax the necroplasma from one prison to the other.

As she chanted the blob finally went still. She completed the spell and willed the necroplasma to move left. When it complied she gave herself a mental high-five. A second command moved it to the opposite side of the circle.

So far so good. Now was when it might get tricky. Using her thumb she rubbed out a portion of the spell circle, just enough for the blob to pass through. She commanded it to move into the lantern.

The blob extended a pseudopod out the gap then inched out. It oozed over to the lantern and stopped.

It fought her control. It was nothing but a fist-sized gob of mindless evil and it still resisted her. Terra ground her teeth and focused all her will on the necroplasma.

"Do it, now!"

With a final quiver the blob entered the lantern. Terra slid the glass back in place and relaxed. The pressure in her mind receded and she let out the breath she'd been holding.

The blob slammed back and forth in its new prison, but her work had paid off. It couldn't escape.

Terra allowed herself ten minutes to recover from the transfer then grabbed the lantern and headed for Chief Kane's office. It was already late afternoon, but she knew he'd want an update at once.

The moment she stepped out of the elevator the chief's secretary waved her through. Terra pushed through the doors and found her boss standing at the window staring out over the city. It was pretty, with a fresh coating of snow over everything.

She'd only been vaguely aware of the weather since she'd been sleeping in her office while she worked on the lantern.

"Sir?"

Orin turned to face her. He was nothing more than a silhouette standing in front of the bright window. "Please tell me you have some good news."

"Well, I'm not sure if it's good or not, but I finished the artifact and transferred the necroplasma. We can begin the hunt first thing in the morning."

He stepped away from the window and sat in his chair. This crisis had aged him. There were new lines around his eyes and she was certain he'd lost weight.

"That's something. Are you certain you can't start today?"

She shook her head. "Too close to nightfall. If we have to deal with shadow beasts it'll be better to do it in the daylight. Besides, I'm so tired I can't see straight. I'll get a good night's sleep and be ready to go in the morning."

He rubbed his face. "Of course. I didn't mean to sound unreasonable. It's just I need this sorted, sooner rather than later."

"I think we all feel that way, at least I know I do. But there's only so much you can do in a day." She debated saying more then shrugged. "Why don't you have an early quit, sir? Go home, see Shizuku, take a little rest. No offense, but you look like hell."

His laugh held no amusement. "That's better than I feel. I have some things to finish up then I'll head out, okay?"

"Yes, sir."

* * *

Lin, Terra, and Clair were gathered in the chief's office. Light poured through the window in an almost blinding glare. On the desk the blob in Terra's lantern was still for once. The nasty thing didn't like the sun. Lin wasn't all that thrilled to see it this morning either. It meant it was hunting time again and so far he hadn't been much use when dealing with these supernatural threats. Other than shooting a few zombies he'd been more hindrance than help.

Chief Kane peered at the lantern then looked up at them. "So this thing's going to lead you to Mercia?"

"That's the theory according to Conryu's scholomantic," Terra said. "I'm in no way ashamed to admit that this is all outside my area of expertise. However, given my complete lack of other ideas, I didn't know what else to try."

"Don't give it a second thought. All avenues must be explored." Chief Kane opened a drawer in his desk and pulled out a long box. "Lin, this is for you."

The chief opened the box revealing a shiny silver pistol and six full clips. They looked like 9mm, the same as his service weapon.

"Thank you, sir, but I'm more familiar with my current weapon."

Chief Kane thumbed one of the cartridges out of its clip and tossed it to Lin. "Look at the bullet."

Lin squinted at the tip. There was something drawn on it. "Sir?"

"Those are rune-marked bullets ordered from Chard Manufacturing: magic bullets. I understand your weapon has been less than effective in your previous outings so I made arrangements for an upgrade. The pistol is designed to handle the bullet's power. A standard weapon would explode the moment you fired it."

Lin looked the bullet over again. An enchanted weapon. With this he would be able to fight and have a hope of accomplishing something instead of hiding and letting Terra handle everything. That idea pleased him a great deal. "Thank you, sir."

Lin swapped his old pistol for the new one then switched out the clips on the opposite side of the holster. The fit was a little tight, but not too bad. The four extra magazines went in his jacket pocket.

"Now." Chief Kane got to his feet. "Go find this psycho and bring her in. I'm not supposed to say this, but if she's not still breathing when you do that's fine."

They left the chief's office and made their way down to the lobby and out to the waiting car. It was, as always lately, a bitterly cold day. Lin couldn't remember a winter this frigid in his forty plus years of living in Sentinel City. He turned the heat all the way up and pulled out of his parking space.

Beside him Terra held her contraption with one hand and touched one of the numerous runes covering it with the other. The lantern lit up and the blob poked up into the glass enclosure.

He drove to the parking lot exit. "What now?"

"Give it a minute," Terra said.

A minute later Lin asked, "What now?"

She glared at him and tapped the lantern glass. The blob wobbled and leaned left. "Go left."

Lin obliged, not daring to go too fast lest he miss a turn. In the back seat Clair snorted. "Do you really think that little ball of snot knows where it's going?"

"If you have a better idea I'd like to hear it," Terra said. "Next right."

Lin made the turn and tried to ignore the ladies' bickering. He had yet to decide if they really didn't like each other or if arguing was just a habit.

For the next hour they drove at an agonizing pace through the crowded city streets, drawing honks and middle-fingers from annoyed drivers. Eventually they left the center of the city behind and headed into the manufacturing district on the outskirts. He drove past a cement factory, then a recycling plant before Terra said, "Stop."

Lin looked out the window at a rundown smelter. It looked like the place hadn't been used in years. A thick layer of soot covered the windows so that he couldn't see anything inside.

"This is the place," Clair said. "I can sense it."

Terra nodded and Lin pulled over and parked on the side of the road. They piled out of the car and stood looking at the huge building.

"You think she's here?" Lin had his doubts. He couldn't imagine anyone living in a place like this.

"Don't judge a book by its cover." Terra held up the lantern and the blob strained to get to the building. "There's definitely something here. With the right magic you could turn the inside into a comfortable residence and no one would know from the outside."

Lin drew his new gun and worked the slide, chambering one of the enchanted bullets. "Well, let's check it out."

* * *

Terra led the group toward the only visible door on this side of the giant factory. The necroplasma struggled to escape, constantly lunging toward the deserted building. The crash of steel getting smashed into cubes at the recycling plant next door made it hard for her to concentrate, but Terra kept the words of a defensive spell on her lips. If this really was Mercia's base then she expected a hard fight.

Terra grabbed the doorknob, but it didn't budge. Lin moved closer, but Clair brushed him out of the way. She chanted in the language of earth and flicked her wrist. The steel-core door ripped free of its hinges and went flying. At least they wouldn't have to worry about anyone barring it behind them and the noise from the plant covered anything they might do.

Clair ducked through first, followed by Terra, with Lin bringing up the rear. The inside stank of grease and burnt metal.

Thin shafts of light filtered through the filthy windows. Terra was afraid to summon fire globes in case something flammable still lingering in the building. It would be a shame to blow themselves up and do Mercia's work for her.

Clair summoned a pair of globes using light magic, revealing a pair of massive crucibles hanging from a system of rails attached to the ceiling. Further down the smelters sat cold and black, like giant lumps of coal.

"What now?" Lin asked.

Terra raised her lantern and watched the blob. It wanted to go deeper into the building so she obliged, easing her way down the soot-covered path between the equipment. An occasional groan or pop echoed through the vast space as the sun heated the cold metal roof. She had to force herself not to look at every squeak and focus on the blob. If there was any threat Clair and Lin would handle it.

The necroplasma grew more frantic the deeper she went until it was positively berserk about a third of the way to the rear of the building near a hydraulic pump that appeared to run the rail system. "We're close. There must be something hidden nearby," Terra said.

Clair cast a seeing spell. The chill in the air changed from physical to psychic. Her casting must have triggered a trap. Something growled from Terra's left followed a moment later by a snarl from her right.

They were surrounded.

"Back to back!" Terra dropped her lantern so she'd be free to cast.

Lin dashed over and stood behind her, his pistol raised and

ready. Clair reached them half a second later. Crystal protrusions covered her like a suit of armor.

From the dark recesses between giant machines, glowing red eyes glared. A trio of hell hounds stepped into the light. Fire dripped from their jaws and black teeth like saliva.

Behind her Lin said, "I have two targets. Do I shoot?"

Terra weighed the risk of blowing them to bits with the risk of getting torn apart. It didn't take long to make up her mind. "Yes."

The word had barely crossed her lips when Lin's pistol cracked followed half a heartbeat later by an even bigger explosion.

As if he'd fired a starting pistol, all hell broke loose. Terra chanted, "Flames of destruction incinerate my enemy, Fire Blast!" and hurled flames.

Clair enchanted a nearby chain and used it to flail at the hell hound nearest her while Lin's pistol cracked again and again.

Terra's first target was pushed back until it slammed into a support column, a huge patch of skin charred and burned away. Despite the damage the hell hound showed no sign of being out of the fight.

The two uninjured hounds gathered themselves.

"Flames of protection appear before me, Fire Wall!" A ten-foot-tall wall of blazing flames sprang up between them and the hounds. "Lin?"

"I took out one, but I needed a full clip to do it. The second one decided to hide behind a pile of scrap. I can't get a clear shot."

Clair shifted and chanted. A loud clatter was followed by explosions and an even louder clatter.

"We're clear on this side." Lin spun to stand at her shoulder.

"I'm lowering the fire wall in three, two, one." She thrust her hands down and the flames vanished.

Behind it the hell hounds were gone.

"Shit! Clair?"

Clair crouched down and rested her palm on the floor while muttering. "They're circling, two left and one right."

"Lin, take the right." Terra raised her hands. "Flames of destruction answer my call."

Blue-white fire danced around her fingers, ready to be hurled at the first sign of the monsters.

"They're coming." Clair straightened and cast a spell of her own. The chain she'd used earlier stiffened into a spear that hung in the air above her.

Lin's pistol spoke first. Terra didn't even have time to glance his way before the remaining two hounds leapt at them. She threw her hands forward, focusing all her power on the nearest demon. The inferno scoured away skin and flesh and bone, leaving nothing but a charred pile of ash.

Clair's spear impaled the second hound and pinned it to the floor. The demon struggled but couldn't free itself.

Terra pointed at the spear. "Light of Heaven burn away this darkness, Lightning Blast."

A crackling bolt of electricity arced down the spear and into the hound, burning it from the inside out until it burst into a puff of black smoke.

"Clear!" Lin said.

Terra wiped the sweat from her brow. They'd survived the first test.

"I have only three clips left," Lin said. "I hope those bullets aren't expensive."

"Only a hundred dollars apiece." Clair bent down and touched the floor again, chanting in the language of earth.

While she was casting Terra retrieved the lantern. Her magic had protected the glass from the drop leaving the necroplasma still trapped and growing more agitated by the second.

"There's a large space under the floor." Clair straightened. "It's three-quarters the size of the factory. I can't get a sense of what's in it."

"Are you being blocked, or is it just too hard to say for sure?" Terra asked.

"There's definitely some sort of ward interfering with my earth magic. All I can tell is a rough idea of size and depth."

"So we're going in blind?" Lin slapped a fresh clip into his pistol.

"Believe it or not," Terra said. "That's a good thing. There must be something important down there if Mercia spent time and magic to protect it."

"I believe it not. If there's one thing I've learned in my years as a cop it's that going into a situation blind is the single most likely thing to get you killed."

"We'll just have to hope you're wrong, because we're going down there just as soon as we find the entrance."

* * *

"Found the release." Clair pulled something behind the pump. A vibration ran through the whole structure as the floor slid open revealing a long staircase.

Terra studied the path down. "I don't see any traps from here."

"I jammed the lever with a piece of scrap." Clair gestured and the light globes flew down the stairs. They'd been hacked out of the bedrock and were far too narrow for Terra's taste. "Those almost look like someone carved them by hand, either that or they were made by an unskilled earth magic wizard. I did better work as a freshman."

Terra looked at Clair. "Do you want to take the lead? You have the best chance of detecting a trap underground."

Clair nodded and started down the steps. Terra followed, picking her way down the narrow path while holding the lantern. The stone had a slight sheen of moisture that made the steps even more treacherous. Lin brought up the rear. When Terra looked back she found him looking over his shoulder more than ahead.

They moved ever deeper into the darkness. Soon the light from behind them vanished and they had nothing but Clair's globes to show them the way. If they had to fight shadow beasts with no sun to weaken them they might be in trouble.

She grit her teeth and kept going. Terra knew going into this it was risky. The three of them would deal with whatever they had to in order to keep Mercia from activating the boxes.

"It levels out up ahead." Clair's voice echoed in the narrow stairway.

Terra picked up her pace and soon she and Lin joined Clair in a wide open space. At the center rested a stone table in a spotlight. "This must be where Mercia sacrificed those unfortunate people to create the necroplasma."

"You were always a clever woman, Terra." Mercia's voice filled the chamber. An illusion of her head appeared in the air above the table. "It's a shame I couldn't be there to greet you in person. We could have had a reunion."

"We know what you're planning and you won't succeed," Terra said.

Mercia laughed. "And who's going to stop me? You three, stuck in a hole with no way out?"

The floor shook as the stairs collapsed, sealing them in. Clair ran back, but flinched away a few feet from the rubble. "There's a dark magic barrier."

"If not us, then someone else. The Department will not let you get away with this." Terra clenched her fists so hard her nails cut into her palm.

"Your faith in your employer is charming, but misplaced. The government doesn't have enough wizards to put out all the fires burning in the Alliance. Once you're dead there will be no one to stand in my way. Have fun playing with my servants." Mercia's head flickered and faded away.

The floor under Terra's feet shook again, harder this time. Lin grabbed the neck of her robe and yanked her back. A second later a black slab shot up to the ceiling followed by another and another. Hundreds of them filled the chamber creating a maze with the table in the center.

"Thanks." Terra straightened her robe.

"No problem. So how do we get out of here?" Lin eyed the imposing black structure and frowned.

"Not the way we came in, that's for sure." Clair joined them near the entrance of the maze. "I couldn't so much as crack the barrier she put up. If we can't dispel it then I can't clear the stairs."

"Our options appear quite limited," Lin said.

"If by that you mean we only have one then I agree."

Terra rubbed the bridge of her nose. "My guess is that table, or perhaps more accurately altar, is the key holding all the wards and constructs down here together. If we destroy it, maybe we have a chance."

"That's a lot of guesses." Clair glared at the maze as if trying to knock it down with sheer force of will.

"Guesses are all I have at this point." Terra set the lantern down and pointed at the necroplasma bouncing around inside. "This thing's done enough damage. Light of Heaven burn away this darkness, Lightning Blast."

A pencil thin beam of electricity shot out, shattered the glass, and incinerated the blob.

"Feel better?" Lin asked.

"Not really. Come on."

* * *

This time Terra took the lead, with Lin in the center and Clair bringing up the rear. Terra claimed it was to allow him to quickly engage an enemy to the front or back, but Lin suspected she just wanted him in the safest place since he was the weakest member of the group. He couldn't even argue. His new gun let him do some damage, but it lacked the versatility of true magic.

All around them warped images followed along. The black stone walls were shiny and reflective, like funhouse mirrors, only without the fun. Everywhere he looked it was like something was moving. Lin didn't know how to separate the false movement from a potentially real threat. He was really starting to regret that transfer just now.

The first turn they came to was a left. Two paces later they reached a three-way intersection. Nothing distinguished one choice from another in his eyes. Terra took the right, looking more confident than he felt.

Lin took one step after her. Another rumble shook the floor and a black panel shot up, separating them from Clair. The maze went pitch black as the light orb died.

Terra hissed a spell and a reddish-orange fireball appeared, filling the air with light. Lin rapped the grip of his pistol on the wall drawing a dull thud.

"Clair!" Terra shouted.

Lin held his breath, but only silence filled the air. Further shouts brought identical results. He groped around where the walls intersected, but they fit so tight he couldn't so much as slip a fingernail between them.

"Shit." Terra slammed her fist into the wall and her fireball flared brighter.

"That sums up our situation beautifully. What now?"

Terra sighed. "We keep moving forward. It's not like we have a lot of other options."

With those words of reassurance they set out once more. Lin stayed as close as possible without stepping on the heels of her shoes. Whatever else happened he didn't want to be trapped alone in the darkness. He was the only one that couldn't make his own light.

"I'm never leaving the car without my flashlight again," he muttered.

"What?"

"Nothing. Think Clair's alright?"

"I hope so. She's a stronger wizard than me so if she's defeated then we're screwed."

"You're not very good at offering reassurances are you?" They came to another intersection and Lin practically draped himself over Terra when they went through it.

"Do you need reassuring?"

An explosion sounded from back the way they'd come. "I do now."

* * *

"Fuck!" Clair slammed her fist into the black slab separating her from Lin and Terra. She made no impression on the unyielding substance. Clair didn't know what the slabs were made of, but it wasn't stone. If Mercia had used rock she'd have knocked the maze flat with a simple spell, as it was, her earth magic didn't so much as touch the stuff.

She ground her teeth and turned her back on the barrier. It wasn't like she didn't have options. There were two other ways to proceed. The question was, which one led her out of this maze?

Straight seemed most likely to take her in the same general direction as her companions so she went that way. Half a dozen steps later a chill presence approached from behind. She spun as a black minotaur lumbered into view. It towered ten feet above her, with curving black horns that sprouted from its bull's head.

Though it was clear what the construct was supposed to be, the minotaur more closely resembled an unskilled child's attempt to make one from clay. The basic shape was correct, but the details were either off or nonexistent. It looked like it was made of pure dark magic, but Clair had never heard of such a thing.

The minotaur stomped the floor and lowered its head. Nothing subtle there.

Clair held her hand palm down. "Oh mother of earth and stone form a weapon to protect your daughter, Earth Spear."

When the minotaur charged Clair punched out at it. The ground shifted and a two-foot-diameter spear of stone burst up through the floor and into the monster's chest.

The force of its charge battled the power of her spell and it was sent flying back. For an instant after impact, the darkness was pushed aside, revealing bronze underneath.

So it wasn't a construct of pure dark magic, but a golem covered in the stuff to protect it from magic. Lucky for her it couldn't protect the statue from impact.

The minotaur picked itself up off the ground, seeming no worse for the tumble. She needed to scrape the dark magic off in order to blast the statue apart. Unfortunately it recovered so fast she didn't have time to cast another spell before the gap she opened sealed itself.

The black statue pawed the ground again. It would drain her, but Clair saw only one option. She placed both hands on the ground. "Oh Mother Earth give birth to a child of stone to serve this unworthy wizard, Stone Behemoth."

The floor shook like an earthquake as a humanoid figure of solid stone pulled itself from the ground. The maze spun around her as she fought the aftereffects of casting two powerful spells in such close succession.

Her behemoth was even cruder in appearance than the minotaur, but it equaled the statue in mass and height. The two constructs came together, fingers locked, chest to chest. Their feet dug into the ground as they pushed and stomped.

It was an even match, but her spell had a limited duration. If she couldn't defeat the minotaur before it ended she'd be on her own again.

The maze finally stopped spinning so she prepared her next spell. She gathered power slowly to avoid another bout of dizziness. Once she was prepared Clair sent a mental command to her behemoth to tear the dark coating off the minotaur.

The stone construct formed a mouth in its crude head and bit into the minotaur's neck. It pulled back with a mouthful of darkness, stretching the covering like rubber until it tore revealing a patch of bronze.

"Shatter and collapse, Earth Breaker." She hurled a shard of earth energy at the exposed metal the moment it appeared.

Her spell struck before the dark magic sealed up. The minotaur trembled. Its left arm and head fell to the floor and smashed to pieces.

What remained of its body continued to struggle. "Crush it, behemoth!"

Massive fists like pile-drivers rose and fell, blasting off chunks of the statue with each impact until nothing remained but a pile of rubble. Only seconds later the behemoth crumbled on top of it. Her spell had lasted just long enough.

Clair slumped to the floor, her body trembling and exhausted.

* * *

The booms and crashes finally ended. Lin wasn't sure if that was a good thing or not and when he'd asked Terra he'd gotten only stony silence in reply. After that he hadn't dared ask if they were lost.

He thought they were. In fact he thought the walls of the maze were shifting behind them. Now that the battle had ended maybe he'd hear if one of the black slabs rose or fell.

They took another right and after fifteen steps came to a dead end. Terra punched the wall then massaged her hand. Lin kept quiet while she paced the narrow path.

When it became painfully obvious she had no idea what to do next he said, "I think the panels are shifting."

"I wouldn't be surprised."

"Their rise and fall is controlled by magic, right?" He was working out his thoughts as he spoke. Lin knew next to nothing about magic so the process was slow.

Terra finally stopped and looked at him. "Yeah, what about it?"

"Well if magic controls them, why can't you mimic the spell to make the one you want go down?"

She opened her mouth then closed it without comment. It was a stupid idea. He should have kept his mouth shut.

"That's not a terrible idea."

Lin must have misheard. "It isn't?"

"In fact it's brilliant. I'm not sure why I didn't think of it myself. Too busy thinking about how to find our way through the maze to consider anything else I guess." She smacked her forehead and muttered a seeing spell. He didn't know what the words meant, but he'd heard them often enough to recognize it.

Terra worked her way slowly along the path, her gaze focused on the junction between the panels and the floor. He wished he could see what she saw, just once.

At last she stopped at the panel blocking their path. "It's so simple I feel like an idiot."

She cast a short spell and dark energy gathered around her hand. She tapped the wall and it slid down into the floor.

"You did it."

She shook her head. "I claim no credit. It was your idea. Let's go."

Terra made a straight line for the center of the maze, tapping each wall as needed to open the way. In less than five minutes the final wall slid down revealing a thirty-by-thirty-yard space with the altar in the middle.

They stepped into the square and Terra nodded. "Just as I thought. All the magic originates from that altar. Once we destroy it the magic holding the panels up will fade along with the barriers."

Lin pointed his pistol at the stone slab, but Terra raised her hand. He lowered his weapon. "What?"

"Your bullets don't have enough punch for this job. I—"

A tortured moan cut her off in mid-sentence. From behind the altar a corpse clambered to its feet and turned to face them. It wore leather biker clothes and had black pits for eyes.

"Does that zombie look familiar?" Lin asked.

"It's one of the Black Skulls and it's not a zombie, there's too much dark energy in it."

Lin gave the undead thing a second look. "If it's not a zombie, what is it?"

The dead Skull leaned toward them like it was about to fall over then it charged, way faster than the zombies he'd fought before.

"Fire Wall!"

The heat from the wall seared Lin's face and forced him to take a step back. The undead burst through the wall of flames with little more than a few scorch marks.

Lin tried to draw a bead on it, but the thing moved too erratically.

He jumped back to avoid a backhand and fired off a pair of rounds. The first missed, but the second hit its left shoulder. The enchanted bullet exploded, tearing a chunk out of it.

Inside the body was flowing darkness like necroplasma.

"Light of Heaven burn away this darkness, Lightning Blast."

Terra's blast sent the creature sailing back through the fire wall. She gestured and the flames vanished. They hadn't been very effective anyway and Lin preferred being able to see.

"You okay?" Terra asked.

He nodded. "Damn, that thing is fast."

The creature had skidded to a stop near the altar. It surged to its feet. The wound he'd put in its shoulder was already closing.

"How do we kill it?" Lin asked.

"Excellent question. Try to take out its legs while I think of an answer."

The undead charged again. How was he supposed to hit something moving like that monster's churning legs? He'd barely hit its body.

He fired a shot at its hip, but it lunged to the side. Lin had its full attention now.

He backpedaled and shot. Fireballs burst all around the thing, but none of them made a solid hit.

It was only yards away, its open mouth revealing inhuman fangs. Lin gave up on its legs and took aim at that open mouth.

Only one shot left so he'd better make it count.

He squeezed the trigger and its head disappeared in a ball of flame.

The still-moving body stumbled past him. Lin ejected his empty clip and slapped a fresh one in. When the smoke around the undead's head cleared it revealed a featureless black oval that immediately sank back into the body.

The undead stopped staggering and oriented on him, the lack of a head seeming to pose no difficulties for it.

Lin had two clips left. Hopefully it would be enough.

* * *

The moment Terra saw the black blob that served as the creature's head she knew what Mercia had done. "Lin, I know how to kill it."

He glanced at her, the relief in his expression palpable. "Don't keep me in suspense."

"You need to blow away the flesh and expose the Faceless One inside so I can sear it away."

Lin grimaced then nodded before returning his full attention to the quickly recovering undead. He raised his pistol and took aim.

"Flames of destruction hear my call." Terra opened a path to the realm of fire. Maintaining it would tire her more quickly, but she wouldn't have to keep chanting the primary phrase each time she wanted to cast her spell, only the words of shaping would be necessary.

Lin fired and the enchanted bullet blew the undead's arm off, revealing the skinny black twig that served the Faceless One.

"Fire Arrow!" She thrust her hand forward and a yard-long bolt of blue flame shot out, incinerating the arm before it withdrew back into the body.

The Faceless One let out a moan. She doubted the thing felt pain, but to have a portion of its essence burned away must have had some effect.

It charged again, this time at her. As Lin said, it was fast, but the damage had slowed it by half a step and she managed to dodge a clubbing blow from its remaining arm.

It stopped to regroup and the moment it did Lin fired again, this time blowing off its right leg below the knee.

"Fire Arrow!" Another section of the monster was burned away.

It bounced in place and flailed with its remaining arm. Lin raised his pistol again, but she lowered it. It couldn't move or attack them now. Terra could finish it herself and save a few of Lin's precious bullets.

Terra raised her hands and sighted through them, centering the bouncing undead. "Flames of deepest earth consume all things in your path. Flames of creation and flames of destruction rise and devour, Volcanic Core!"

The ground shook and a pillar of glowing white flames blasted up through the hobbling monster. Everything was burned away. Flesh, bone, and darkness were all consumed by the pure white flames.

When nothing remained but her own magic in the pyre she lowered her hands and ended the spell. Sweat plastered her hair to her face and she stumbled when she tried to take a step. Lin caught her and eased her to the ground.

"Thanks."

He nodded and sat beside her. "That was impressive. How come you didn't use that spell to start with?"

Terra blew out a sigh. She was right on the edge of backlash. If that spell hadn't ended it they would have been fully screwed. "It's too slow to hit a moving target and I can only cast it once before I need to take a long rest."

"Well, since there's nothing trying to kill us at the moment I'd say you've earned that rest." Lin gave her a pat on the back.

"Thanks, but I'm worried about Clair. It seems like she should have caught up to us by now."

"If she didn't figure out how to lower the panels she's probably still wandering around lost. We certainly would be."

"I guess, but I'm in no shape to do anything about it one way or the other."

* * *

Terra allowed herself a full three hours to recover from the battle. Even in the sunless chamber she had an excellent sense of time. After four years at the academy she'd mastered telling time in her head. It was a necessity if you wanted to arrive anywhere when you were supposed to and a useful trick for wizards, some of whose spells lasted for a specific length.

She climbed to her feet and stretched. The weakness and dizziness had passed and her body felt strong enough to channel magic again. Lin joined her and together they eyed the altar.

"You up to smashing that thing?"

Terra had no intention of admitting it, but she wasn't entirely certain she was up to it. All the room's magic was flowing from the stone out to the maze and barriers. There was bound to be potent protections in place. She would have much preferred to tackle it in combination with Clair, but the other wizard hadn't made it to the central chamber yet. Terra didn't much like Clair, but she was starting to worry.

"One way to find out, right?" Terra rolled up her sleeves, flexed her fingers, and tried to think which spell to use to destroy the altar. Her best hope had to be with fire magic since it was her aligned element, making her twice as powerful in it as any other. Ideally she'd like a dark magic wizard to strip away the wards first, but that was out of the question.

Finally she made up her mind. "Stay back near the wall."

When Lin had moved as far from the altar as possible, she raised her hands and focused her will. "Oh flame of god's forge, swirl, rage, and consume all things, Vulcan's Tornado!"

Heat gathered as Terra spun her hands, shaping the burgeoning fire into a vortex. Over the course of half a minute a full-fledged funnel cloud of flames gathered around the altar. The stone grew red hot, but didn't melt. She needed to kick up the heat.

"Father of winds grant this unworthy servant of fire the loan of your breath, Gust!"

She directed the hot dry winds into a matching vortex. The heat tripled and the edges of the altar liquefied, dripping onto the floor.

Just a little more, oh winds.

In answer to her mental plea the gust grew in intensity. Her enhanced vision revealed the web of magic holding the wards together growing unstable as the stone broke down.

Terra grabbed Lin and dragged him behind the panels. Seconds later the altar exploded. Gravel rained against the makeshift barrier. When all had gone silent they inched their way back into the chamber.

The altar was nothing but a pile of half-melted rock. The wards were fading fast. A minute later all the panels crashed back into the floor. She slumped, but remained on her feet. Terra doubted she could cast another spell today if their lives depended on it.

Lin gave her robe a tug. "There's Clair."

She looked where he indicated. Clair was lying on the hard floor, dead or unconscious Terra couldn't tell. They ran over and Lin knelt and checked her pulse. "She's alive."

"Backlash. She must have had one hell of a fight."

"What now?"

"Now we rest. No way are we getting out of here before tomorrow at the earliest. If I have to clear all the rubble myself it might take two days.

* * *

In the end it took a day and a half for the tired, hungry, and thirsty people to dig their way out. Lin carried the still-unconscious Clair out of the factory and to their car. Terra followed along behind in only slightly better shape.

He started the car and cranked the heat before pulling out and heading back to the Department. The return trip went way quicker and twenty minutes later they were parked and Lin was carrying Clair in to the infirmary. He put her on the hard cot and Terra covered her with the thin rags that passed for blankets.

"How long do you think she'll be out?" Lin asked.

Terra shrugged. "No idea. Wizards handle backlash differently. I'm surprised she hasn't woken up already. If she doesn't wake up in another day they'll have to put in an IV to keep her from getting dehydrated. The longest backlash coma I've ever seen lasted three weeks and the wizard couldn't cast for six months."

"Let's hope Clair isn't out of commission for that long. I have a strong feeling we're going to need her before six months are up."

Chapter 7

Removing the Brand

Conryu eyed the most recent target Mrs. Lenore had prepared for them. It looked like a bowling ball someone had covered with geometric designs. On the other side of the classroom Mrs. Lenore was giving the girls some instructions for their training. He didn't pay any attention since he was never going to have to do circle casting.

For the past month he and Kelsie had obliterated everything she'd put in front of them with no discernible difficulties. In fact their practice time lasted less than five minutes at the start of each class. It was yet more going through the motions, but at least it was fast. As soon as they finished he'd settle in with his Infernal study guide and Prime would help him practice telepathically. Having a demon as a study buddy made learning the awkward language much easier.

Beside him Kelsie was fidgeting and trying to focus on Mrs. Lenore's instructions while darting glances at today's target. Every time it seemed she was afraid they'd fail. So far they hadn't, but if they did he feared she'd blame herself.

"Will you relax? If you tense up your power won't flow as easily."

"Really?"

He had no idea if that was true, but she was making him nervous and that wasn't helpful. "Yes, now calm down. Try the backwards counting trick."

She fell into the easy breathing rhythm he'd taught her and soon her fidgeting stopped. She couldn't have gotten past twenty numbers when Mrs. Lenore came to join them. The rest of the class was up to four-person circles and she seemed very pleased with their progress.

The moment she stopped in front of Kelsie and Conryu her smile vanished. She'd been trying for weeks to find something that would challenge them and so far had come up short.

"So whose bowling ball are we sacrificing?" Conryu asked.

"It's not a bowling ball, it's an earth density orb. The earth magic seniors use them to practice altering the density of stone without changing its mass. This one has had its density maxed out. I doubt a drill with a diamond bit would scratch it."

"Cool. Anyone ever try to blast one of these things with dark magic before?"

"Not as far as I know. If you two destroy the orb, that's it. I have no idea what else to give you as a target."

"We still have three and a half months of school left," Kelsie said. "What will we do for the rest of the semester?"

"You'll work on circle casting and he can work on whatever Angeline, that is Mrs. Umbra, has him practicing."

Conryu rubbed his hands together. "Let's crack this egg. Ready, partner?"

Kelsie gave the orb a dubious look then took her place behind Conryu. When her hand settled in place Conryu began the spell. "Darkness bind our power as one, Break and Shatter!"

The ebony ray lanced out and struck the orb. It resisted for an instant before crumbling to gravel. Conryu grinned and thrust a fist into the air. "Yes!"

Mrs. Lenore's shoulders slumped. "I thought I had you for half a second there. Congratulations, you two can officially handle anything you'll encounter in the final."

Kelsie went and joined a circle while he settled in to study. Prime's telepathic voice appeared in his head. *You could have destroyed that orb on your own. That girl is unnecessary.* The scholomantic sounded the same whether it spoke out loud or mentally.

Conryu still had to mutter, but he could keep his voice low enough so the others didn't hear, not that they'd be apt to, given their chanting. "I suspected as much, but I'd appreciate it if you didn't run down my partner."

Prime's disdain came clearly through their link, but the scholomantic refrained from further comment. They spent the next hour and a half in mental conversation. He got comfortable with a handful of new words before everyone left him to wait for Mrs. Umbra.

She tapped her way in five minutes later. "I trust you two have been practicing the summoning spell?"

"Yeah, we can manage about fifty yards now. But I've been worried lately about what will happen if Lucifer senses Prime passing through the gate and grabs him."

"The transition over such a short distance is instantaneous. It would be like trying to pluck a bullet out of midair with your bare hands."

"I get that, but I'd feel a lot better if we removed this stupid brand from my arm."

She sat on the edge of Mrs. Lenore's desk. "As would I, but I haven't come up with any way of doing it."

"What if I just forced Lucifer to take it off himself? After all he put it there."

"That's a bold plan, but I fear you're not strong enough even knowing the domination spell." She tapped the head of the Death Stick on her palm. "But maybe if I teach you how to use this."

* * *

Despite the cold Conryu and Mrs. Umbra left the nice warm school and walked down to the beach. She informed him there was no way he was starting his practice inside since she didn't want him bringing the building down on them when he screwed up. Which he would, since everyone screwed up their first time using a magical artifact to enhance their casting.

They stopped at the edge of the frozen lake. He couldn't stop his teeth from chattering so he didn't know how he'd cast a spell. Mrs. Umbra took pity on him and hissed a fire spell. Warmth rushed into him and he sighed.

"So what do you want me to do first?"

"I want you to listen while I explain how this works. The Death Stick allows a dark-aligned wizard to channel twice as much energy as they'd be able to otherwise. You understand the implications for you?"

Conryu shook his head. He didn't fully understand what all the numbers they used to describe power levels meant. He used magic more instinctively than intellectually.

"I'll use myself as an example. If I were to take the wizard's test again I'd pull around 3,000 as a base and 6,000 in dark magic. If I channel through the Death Stick that dark magic number goes up to 12,000, making me one of the most powerful dark magic users in the world."

"Wow."

"I'm not saying that to impress you." He flinched at her angry tone. "I need you to understand. My maximum power is a hair lower than your base. If you use the Death Stick your dark magic potential approaches 50,000, four times greater than mine."

"Sure, that's a lot, but the numbers don't mean anything to me. They're just words."

"Let me put it this way. If you cast Dispel with the Death Stick you could probably negate every spell and ward on campus."

Conryu's jaw dropped. "Holy shit. Seriously?"

"Seriously. That's why we're going to proceed with great caution. Any spell you cast will be directed out over the lake and away from the school. You want to try it?"

He swallowed the lump in his throat. If he wanted to force Lucifer to remove the brand he needed to figure this out. "Let's do it."

She handed him the Death Stick and the handle vibrated in his grip. When he told her, Mrs. Umbra said, "It's responding to your magical potential. The vibration's in your mind not your hand. Don't worry, it's a good sign. The artifact has accepted you as a viable user. That's the first step."

"Right, okay. What would have happened if it rejected me?"

"Nothing. You would have felt no vibration and when you cast it wouldn't have enhanced your spell. The Death Stick only responds to those with a dark magic potential over 5,000. Now, we're going to start with a spell you're familiar with." She pointed out over the lake toward the island. "I want you to cover the island in Cloak of Darkness."

The island had to be over a mile long. He'd only ever covered himself and Prime in the cloak. "The whole thing?"

"Yes. Remember, don't think you can, know you can."

Right, he had to believe it was possible to have any hope of getting the spell to work. He took a breath and settled himself. When he spoke the first word of the spell it felt like someone had breached a dam. Power unlike anything he'd ever imagined rushed into him.

He focused through the rush and finished the spell, waving the Death Stick towards the island as he did so. Liquid darkness fell across three-quarters of the island before the last of the energy left him. He felt hollowed out. He'd never experienced anything like it.

When he described it to Mrs. Umbra she nodded. "That's not uncommon when using an artifact. Wait until you cast a spell without it for the first time. It'll feel like the most pitiful thing ever. Don't worry, it's only because of the proportion. You're not any weaker."

He looked out over the mostly covered island. "I couldn't cover the whole thing."

She laughed. "I didn't think you could. In fact I doubted you'd manage half, so this is better than I expected. With time and practice you'll be able to draw out the Death Stick's full potential."

Conryu recalled the massive power and shook his head. "That wasn't full strength?"

Mrs. Umbra's face crinkled when she smiled. "You only tapped a little over half your maximum. When you reach one hundred percent I doubt you'll have any trouble convincing Lucifer to remove your brand."

* * *

Conryu watched as Crystal adjusted the runes covering the piston and cylinder. Her earth magic created oil with no trouble, just way too much. He wasn't concerned though. If there was one thing working on Blinky had taught him, it was to expect to make adjustments. They'd been working on the engine every Sunday for six weeks now.

Sonja had inscribed a steel cylinder with fire magic to replace the spark plug. Once Crystal fixed the lubrication problem he'd reassemble the motor and see if it worked or if they'd made a bomb.

"So what are you guys studying now?" Sonja asked. The two of them were keeping their distance so Crystal could better focus.

"Nothing but Infernal in my regular class, but Mrs. Umbra is teaching me how to use the Death Stick."

She perked up at that. "Third year my class got to try the Ashen Scepter, but I didn't have a strong enough potential to make it work. Actually only one girl in my class succeeded in awakening it and she's a prodigy. Like you I guess."

129

Conryu laughed at that. He was no more a prodigy than he was a duck. "Is this the girl you couldn't beat at the team tryouts?"

"Yeah. Her fire magic potential is the strongest in a hundred years so I don't feel bad about it."

He nodded. "It was pure chance I was born with enough power to wield the artifact. Mrs. Umbra says only someone with dark magic potential over 5,000 can use it. I've still only managed to draw out about three-quarters of its full strength."

Sonja patted his knee. "Just keep at it. If anyone can master it, you can."

"Thanks." The little fire wizard's vote of confidence meant a lot to him. It surprised Conryu how much he'd come to value Sonja after such a short time knowing her. Maybe it was because she acted more like a middle-schooler sometimes than she did a twenty-two-year-old that made him protective of her.

"I think I have it," Crystal said.

Sonja sprinted over to the workbench and he joined her a moment later. Conryu ran his finger down the piston. There was just a thin sheen covering it. When he checked the fit in the cylinder it slid in and out without any friction.

"What do you think?" Sonja was bouncing in place.

"I think when I finish putting it back together we can test it."

"Yes!" Sonja jumped up and spun around.

An hour later the engine was reassembled and sitting upright in the cradle he'd built for it. "So how do we start this thing?" he asked.

Sonja hopped up on a stool to get a better look. "See that big rune beside the fire cylinder?"

"Yeah."

"When you touch it a link will be created between you and the engine. Your magic will power it the same way you maintain a spell like seeing, though this will drain you faster than such a basic spell."

"That's it?" It sounded too simple.

"That's it. Bear in mind that what seems like no big deal for you would exhaust me in half an hour. That's why a magic engine really isn't practical for most people. A non-wizard couldn't even use it."

"Cool." He touched the rune.

A little jolt ran through him and the engine fired. The piston cycled and turned the drive shaft. He let it run for half a minute. It looked like Sonja had it set for about a hundred rpm. Nowhere near enough to make it useful, but enough to prove the concept. As a nice bonus it didn't blow up and kill them all.

"How do I switch it off?"

"Touch the rune again."

Conryu did so and the engine shut off. A little tingle passed through him as the link vanished. "I'd call that a successful test. You know what we need to do now?"

Sonja's smile had her face stretched tight. "What?"

"Build something for it to run. Maybe a go cart or dirt bike."

"I vote go cart." Sonja was waving her arms around. "All of us can ride in that."

"If you guys think I'm getting in anything powered by an experimental magic engine you're both nuts," Crystal said.

Sonja and Conryu shared a look. "So a two-seater?" he asked.

She grinned and they bumped fists.

* * *

Conryu bounded down the stairs and into his room. He'd left Prime in the library and now he was going to try and summon him. He'd managed the spell over shorter distances, but the library was right at the outer limit of their link. If this worked he could summon Prime from anywhere.

He cleared his mind and focused on the tether that connected him to the scholomantic. He pictured it as a black thread running from his chest to Prime's spine. When he had the link fully visualized he took a breath.

Before he spoke the first word of the spell someone knocked. Conryu blew out a sigh. He wasn't expecting anyone. He sent a thought of patience to Prime and opened the door. Maria was waiting outside and hanging her head.

"Hey, what's up?"

She slipped past him and sat on the edge of his bed. When she finally looked up he took a step back. A full beard covered her face.

"Holy shit! What happened to you?"

She sniffed back a tear. "In alchemy club I reversed the order of two ingredients and the potion blew up in my face. You can see the results."

"Yeah. What are you going to do about it?"

Maria gave him the most pathetically hopeful look. "I thought maybe you could use dark magic to negate the potion's effect."

Conryu winced. Maria was highly sensitive to dark magic so if she was willing to have him use it on her she must have been desperate. The problem was he had no idea if Dispel would work on something like this and if he used breaking he might blow her head off. Delicate magic was in no way his strong suit.

"Maybe we should ask Mrs. Lenore. Having me blast you willy-nilly with dark magic might not be the best idea."

"No!" She grabbed his arm before he could take a step toward the door. "Bad enough the alchemy class knows I screwed up the potion, but no one knows about the beard but you. I took off as soon as I felt it start growing."

He understood how she wouldn't want anyone to know about this. He snapped his fingers. "I bet Prime will know what to do. I was just about to try summoning him. Hang on."

Conryu moved as far from Maria as the room would permit and repeated the visualization process. When he was ready he chanted, "Come to me through darkest paths, Familiar Summons!"

A black disk appeared in the air and Prime emerged through it before it shut. "Well done, Master. Even that terrifying witch will be impressed with this."

"Thanks, but we have a more pressing problem."

Prime flew over and studied Maria from head to toe. "This was caused by a misfired potion, yes?"

She nodded.

"It can't be dispelled by dark magic. You either need to use the correct counter-potion or wait for the effects to end. It shouldn't last more than a week."

"A week!"

Prime flew around behind him. "At most. It might only last three or four days."

"Why can't we dispel it?" Conryu asked.

Prime peeked over his shoulder at the still-fuming Maria. "Potion magic works by infusing power into a person's entire body. It's not just a matter of zapping her face. You'd have to remove every trace of the magic from her entire body without damaging her cells. No offense, Master, but you still lack sufficient control for such a delicate operation."

He couldn't argue with that. While his control had improved he would never dare anything that delicate, especially on Maria, with her low tolerance for dark magic. "Maybe there's another option."

Maria perked up. "Anything."

Conryu ducked into his bathroom and returned with his disposable razor. "You could shave."

She stared at him for a moment. "Shave? That's your brilliant idea?"

"I didn't say it was brilliant, but there's a long tradition of using these to remove facial hair. It has to be safer than me blasting you in the face with dark magic."

She crossed the room and took the razor from him. "I guess it couldn't hurt to try."

Five minutes later she emerged, clean shaven, from the bathroom. "How do I look?"

"Gorgeous. How's it feel?"

"The skin's a little sensitive, but other than that not bad."

"Cool. You can keep the razor if you want."

"Thanks, but I have a pack in my room."

An image of Maria shaving her legs in the shower popped unbidden into his head. He sighed and shook it off. "I forgot to tell you. We got the engine running."

"That was fast. I thought it would take you longer to figure out how to replicate all the mechanical issues."

"We simplified everything so all that was left was basically the cylinder, piston, and drive shaft. Next week we're going to start working on a go cart."

She smiled. "If you were half as enthusiastic about magic as you were about your toys, you'd be the greatest wizard since—"

"Don't say it."

"Merlin."

* * *

Conryu couldn't stop pacing as he waited for Mrs. Umbra to arrive. Three days ago he'd managed to cover the entire island in Cloak of Darkness and she pronounced him ready to confront Lucifer. He'd been eager at the time, but now that the moment was here, fear had replaced excitement.

After another ten trips up and down the aisle he stopped and sat on the nearest desk. He needed to follow the advice he always gave Kelsie. Slow breaths. Focus on the goal. He knew what he was capable of when using the Death Stick. He'd pop in to Hell, force Lucifer to remove the brand, and be back before he knew it.

Right. That's why he hadn't mentioned anything to Maria over dinner last night. At least her beard had stopped growing. Thinking about those soft, smooth cheeks covered in thick, bristly hair brought a smile to his face and eased his nerves.

It was easy for him to think of Maria as perfect when it came to schoolwork so it was heartening that even she made an occasional mistake. Not that she saw it that way, but with a perfectionist you had to make allowances.

When Mrs. Umbra finally arrived he'd calmed down enough to think he had a chance of succeeding. A frown made her wrinkles deepen. "Are you certain you want to go through with this? The risks are tremendous."

"I know, but the risk of doing nothing and then having to travel by dark portal... I don't know. As long as I know he's just waiting on the other side for me to arrive makes it hard to concentrate on anything else. I need to do this as much to get it off my mind as anything else."

She nodded and held the Death Stick out to him. "I understand. I'll prepare the circle, you work on strengthening your link to the artifact."

Conryu focused all his attention on the Death Stick. What had once been a vibration when he first picked it up had now evolved into an almost electric current running between them. It approached the intensity of his connection to Prime.

While Mrs. Umbra drew on the floor he did the visualization exercises she'd taught him. Over and over again he imagined the enhanced domination spell overwhelming Lucifer and forcing him to obey.

Sometime later he was brought back to reality when Mrs. Umbra said. "We're ready."

He opened his eyes and studied the spell circle she'd drawn. It was different than before, simpler. When he commented on it she said, "It's a simple portal containment spell. You're not going to form a contract after all."

"Right, so is there some way for me to retreat if this doesn't work?" When he'd gone to form a contract with Cerberus he couldn't return unless he succeeded. That was pressure he didn't need while dealing with Lucifer.

"Don't worry, I left an escape valve this time. Just say 'return' in Infernal and you'll be yanked back to our reality."

"That's a relief, not that I intend to fail."

"No one intends to fail, but it still happens. Good luck."

She patted him on the knee as he and Prime stepped into the center of the circle. He touched the Death Stick to the central rune and willed it to activate.

He blinked and found himself surrounded by darkness. A rough, dry tongue licked his left cheek while a giant head rubbed his right side.

"Good boy." Conryu rubbed Cerberus behind the ears and the giant demon dog groaned like a puppy. He really needed to introduce Cerberus to Kelsie. If she saw him like this she wouldn't be at all afraid of him.

Cerberus's heads all popped up and a deep growl rumbled through his chest. Something moved out in the darkness. "It's okay, boy. I was expecting him."

Cerberus whined and Conryu knew how he felt. Just because he was expecting Lucifer didn't mean he was looking forward to the confrontation.

When he could make out the horns on the demon's head he began the domination spell. "By my will be bound, oh child of Hell. Your thoughts are my thoughts, your desires, my desires, Domination!"

The massive power gathered in the Death Stick by his spell lashed out and crashed into Lucifer's mind. Unlike the weaker demons he'd subjugated, the Prince of Lies resisted with more strength than even Conryu had expected.

Lucifer clutched his skull, his handsome, arrogant face twisted in pain. Over and over in his mind Conryu commanded the demon to submit.

Lucifer snarled. "You think you can command me, mortal. Me! Who is more akin to a god than a demon. I will break your spell and rend you limb from limb."

Conryu ignored the threats and continued to press his commands with everything he had. Lucifer continued to resist just as fiercely.

Cerberus's head brushed his hand and a jolt of power ran through him and out into Lucifer as the demon dog joined his will to Conryu's.

Lucifer howled and thrashed. For a moment he feared their combined power wouldn't be enough. Then Lucifer's face went slack and the spell settled into place.

Conryu didn't dare let out so much as a sigh of relief lest he break his fragile spell. "Remove your brand from my arm."

He raised his arm and pulled the sleeve of his robe back revealing the mark underneath. Lucifer raised his trident like a zombie and waved it over Conryu's arm. The mark burned even worse for a second then it was gone.

"Leave this place and never show yourself before me again." He combined that command with an overwhelming desire for Lucifer to be gone.

The giant demon fled back the way he'd come as fast as he could fly. Conryu held the Death Stick up and ready until Lucifer had moved fully beyond his sight. Only then did he release the sigh he'd been holding back.

"That was impressive." Soft hands massaged his shoulders while a tail wrapped around his thigh and worked its way up toward his groin.

They'd been so focused on Lucifer neither he nor Cerberus had noticed the Dark Lady's approach. That she hadn't interfered was a point in her favor, but she was still a demon.

Conryu pulled away and spun to face her, the Death Stick between them.

She raised her hands and her perfect lips curled into a smile. "I have no wish to fight you. Your display with Lucifer got me all excited." She ran her hands down her breasts and stomach.

Conryu had more trouble concentrating now than he did when Lucifer burned his mark off. "What do you want?"

Her lips parted revealing elongated eyeteeth. "I want to be your friend, your special friend."

He raised an eyebrow at that. If Maria was jealous of him and Kelsie how would she react to him being special friends with the Dark Lady? "I'm not really looking to form another demon contract. Cerberus is a fine partner and Prime is an outstanding familiar."

Cerberus barked once as if in agreement. She glowered at him prompting the demon dog to shy away and whimper. "I can offer you far more than these limited allies you've chosen."

He allowed himself another long look at her perfect figure. That brought her smile back.

"I know you desire me, mortal. Accept me in Cerberus's place and I shall give you pleasure beyond anything you can conceive of. We can seal the bargain with a kiss."

She leaned in, her lips glistening. Conryu's head swam and he couldn't focus. This was wrong, but for the life of him he couldn't figure out why.

Prime flew in front of him, blocking off his view of the Dark Lady. The moment he did Conryu's mind cleared.

Bitch! She'd used some sort of magic on him. "Cloak of Darkness."

The anti-magic coating covered him and Prime a moment before the scholomantic went flying. When she saw Conryu covered in darkness the Dark Lady bared her fangs and hissed. "You would have had much more fun if you'd just played along."

"I will not be your slave." He raised the Death Stick between them and held his free hand out for Prime.

Her expression smoothed as though nothing had happened. "Perhaps I was a bit forward. It is my nature after all. What if we tried something else, sort of a getting to know you phase. I could be your agent. All powerful dark wizards need a demonic agent to keep them abreast of what's happening in Hell. If I was your agent I wouldn't be able to work against you."

Prime slapped into his hand, but he never took his eyes off the Dark Lady. "What's in it for you?"

She pressed a hand over her heart. "I only want to help."

"Then don't lie to me. If you say there's nothing in this for you then I call bullshit. You're looking for a power boost."

"Such a charming mortal expression. Fine, I want a power boost. The stronger the wizard the more powerful I become. Why do you think Lucifer was so eager to kill you after you refused him?"

"He didn't want anyone else to form a contract with me and grow stronger."

She nodded. "With your power you'd have your pick of demonic servants. Now that you've cut ties with Lucifer others will come calling. With me as your agent you'll have someone to warn you when the next one decides to try and strike a bargain."

Conryu lowered the Death Stick slightly. If she was telling the truth there was certainly something to her suggestion. It was simply too much for him to decide in his exhausted state.

She seemed to sense his wavering and leaned closer, giving an up-close look at her exquisite chest. "I have much to offer."

No kidding. "I'll think about it. Return!"

In a blink he and Prime were back in the dark magic classroom. Returning to the real world drained the last of his strength. He wobbled and barely made it to a nearby chair before his legs gave out.

"Is it done?" Mrs. Umbra hobbled over to him and reclaimed the Death Stick from his nerveless fingers.

"Yeah, but there's something else we need to discuss when I'm less exhausted."

"My office, after the evening meal tomorrow."

He nodded and fell asleep in the chair.

* * *

Conryu's head throbbed, though he was pretty sure it wasn't from magical backlash. He was sitting in the cafeteria waiting for Maria to join him for dinner. The voices of the other students chattering about this and that, none of it remotely serious, set his nerves on end. What he wouldn't have given to talk to Jonny for an hour about sports or bikes or just about anything besides magic or demons. He might as well have wished to visit the moon, he had about as much chance of having that granted.

He'd woken up half an hour ago in the dark magic classroom, alone and with a blanket draped over him. He'd have to remember to thank Mrs. Umbra tomorrow, which brought him back to the source of his current headache. Despite his most earnest wish to have as little to do with the politics of magic as possible he kept getting dragged deeper into it.

Between the Department and the Dark Lady's warning it was like he'd gotten stuck in quicksand. At least whatever they were serving tonight smelled good. He was about to check it out when Maria pushed through the doors. She waved and smiled, making her way over to join him at their usual table.

"Have you been waiting long? I was practicing bone fusions and totally lost track of time."

"I've been here maybe fifteen minutes. How's your...?" He brushed his cheek with his index finger.

"Not a single hair in twenty-four hours. I think it's run its course. Thank goodness for that. What about you? You're looking a little rough around the edges."

"It was an eventful afternoon." He filled her in on his confrontation, careful to keep his voice low. It wasn't necessarily a secret that he was having demon issues, but he didn't want to announce it to the whole world either. When he finished Maria was staring at him. "I'm supposed to talk to Mrs. Umbra tomorrow about the whole agent thing. Do you know anything about it?"

Maria shook her head. "Mom never wanted to get mixed up in politics, either human or spirit. It's one of the reasons she doesn't work for the Department. That and private practice pays better."

"I never wanted to get mixed up in it either, but from the sound of it, now that I've chased off Lucifer, I'm going to have a bunch of other demons looking to make use of my power. I swear I wish I could rip this power out of my body and stick it in someone else."

Maria reached out and took his hand. "I'm glad you're the one who got it. I know you don't want it, but can you imagine what someone inclined to evil could accomplish with your magic? The world should be grateful someone as kind and honorable as you were born with it."

Conryu kissed her cheek. "Thanks. Let's find something to eat."

They collected their food and while they ate Maria told him about her studies. She'd healed a bird's wing, enabling it to fly again. Only her and two others had succeeded at that complex ritual. He smiled as she went on and on in fine detail as only Maria could when she was fully engrossed in a subject.

Her absolute delight in her studies was infectious and his headache faded away. She said it was lucky that he was born with the power, but Conryu thought it would have been much better if Maria had been the one to get it. On the other hand, he doubted she would be as happy if she had to spend her afternoons in Hell or worrying about whether the religious nuts, the crazy wizards, or the devil would be the one to succeed in murdering her.

The thought of Maria having to deal with all that made him glad, just for a second, that he was the one with the power and not her.

* * *

As Conryu made his way upstairs to Mrs. Umbra's office he wondered for the hundredth time why he bothered going to dark magic class at all. He sat there for two hours watching the girls doing circle casting and studying Infernal with Prime. He gained nothing from the former and could easily do the latter in the library or his room.

If nothing else he could now carry on a reasonable conversation in the demonic language. He wasn't fluent yet, but he was getting there. Mrs. Umbra's door opened at his approach. It was like the doors at the grocery store only with magic instead of electronics. Probably shouldn't make the comparison to his teacher.

Mrs. Umbra was seated behind her desk scowling at the Death Stick which rested in front of her. She looked up when he entered and waved him to an empty chair.

"Everything okay?" He settled into the guest seat.

"I'm just reminding this ungrateful artifact who its proper master is. You spoiled it and now it's trying to refuse my magic."

"Sorry."

She waved him off. "It's fine. I sorted it out, but you can't use it again. If you do I fear there'll be no getting it back."

"I didn't want to use it the first time, but circumstances forced my hand."

"Shit happens, as the kids like to say. So what's so important?"

He gave her the gist of his conversation with the Dark Lady. "She seems to think other demons are going to come calling. I'd really like to dismiss that out of hand, but I can't. Everything she said makes too much sense.

"You're right and I should have considered the repercussions of driving off Lucifer more closely. That said, I don't see any alternative to removing his brand since he kept trying to kill you."

"Agreed. But that begs the question of whether I need an agent in Hell or not. Do you have one?"

"I do. An imp I call Zippy because he's always flitting around like a humming bird. He keeps me abreast of what's happening in a general way, armies of demons gathering, two of the princes going to war, that sort of thing. Zippy doesn't have the access to find out detailed plots so he's less useful than he might be. I made the deal with him when I was young and never bothered ending it."

"So what should I do? Do I take the Dark Lady up on her offer or do I find an imp or some other minor demon?"

"An imp wouldn't do you any good." She sighed. "I hate to let that harpy get a single talon into you, but I fear she's your best bet. You're already partially connected anyway. If you form a proper contract she'll be unable to take any action against you and likewise you'll be unable to harm her."

"I wasn't planning on trying to harm her." In fact he'd prefer to have nothing at all to do with her.

"I know, so the contract gains you a great deal and costs you nothing. I'll write it up for you like I did with Cerberus then you can copy it and show it to her during our next class."

"You're going to have to teach me that spell circle you use so you won't have to keep drawing it for me."

"Your book should have the circle, it's a standard spell." She snapped her fingers. "That's your homework. Memorize the circle so you can draw it when we meet the day after tomorrow."

That'd teach him to open his big mouth.

* * *

Conryu appeared once again on the border of Hell, contract in hand. He'd drawn the circle to Mrs. Umbra's satisfaction on the first try, which both pleased and surprised him. As always Cerberus was on the other side waiting for him. The demon dog seemed anxious and he suspected he knew why.

He scratched the central head behind the ear. "Don't worry, I'm not going to end our contract. She's going to be busy spying on the other demons so your job isn't in danger."

Cerberus barked and gave him a playful butt with his right head. Conryu laughed and gave him a swat on the flank.

"A boy and his dog, how sweet." The Dark Lady appeared from above and to his right. Her flimsy black dress swirled around her as her wings flapped and she landed in front of him. "I assume you've considered my offer."

"I did. Here's my counteroffer." He handed her the contract.

The Dark Lady's expression went from cool to bright and back again as she read the various clauses Mrs. Umbra had included. The whole thing was only a page long. She said the simpler the contract the less chance a wily demon might find something to pervert to her benefit.

At last she lowered the paper and looked at him. "This is more generous and detailed than I expected. I assume you had help writing it?"

"I consulted a more experienced wizard, yes. So is it a deal?"

"It is. With this I'll move into the upper echelon of Hell." She scratched her finger and let a drop of thick black blood drip onto the paper.

A cord of power shot from his chest to hers. For a moment his mind was overwhelmed with visions of lust and power. Every act of domination or perversion conceivable flooded into him. There was no rhyme or reason to it, just a riot of images coming and going so fast he could hardly separate one from the next.

It was over in seconds. When he recovered his wits he found the Dark Lady licking her lips and smiling. Her presence had expanded, that was the only way to describe the feeling he got when he looked at her. The contract had served its purpose and been consumed.

"Was that your mind I saw?"

"Only the tiniest piece of it." She glided closer and rested her hands on his shoulders, her face just inches from his. "I could teach you so much more. You've only scratched the surface of your capability. It's going to be a dark and glorious journey, Master. I am eager to begin."

"You're eager to show off your new power."

Her smile grew and her grip tightened. "I can't keep any secrets from you, can I. You're right. I'm looking forward to returning to the Black City and putting several of my ill-mannered former peers in their proper place. With the power I've gained it will not be difficult."

"How much has our bargain increased your strength?"

"I'm half again as powerful as I was. Alas, you won't receive a similar boost. Your gains will be much more focused. You will find spells that affect the minds of your targets simpler and more potent than they otherwise would be. That is my area of expertise after all." She leaned closer and kissed his cheek. "Call me some evening, Master, and I will be happy to instruct you."

Prime flew closer. "I will handle the master's instruction."

The Dark Lady flicked a glance at the scholomantic and immediately dismissed him. Conryu had the impression using magic was the last thing she planned to instruct him in.

He needed to move this conversation in a different direction. "How will you contact me if there's a threat?"

"In your dreams. When your mind is free our link will allow me to create a lucid dream where we can interact."

"Okay, good luck. Return!"

He was once more back in the classroom. Mrs. Umbra was staring at him while leaning on the Death Stick. "How'd it go?"

"She accepted and seemed well pleased with the terms. She plans to use her newfound power to put some rivals in what she considers their proper place."

Mrs. Umbra snorted. "Typical demonic behavior. You've made a lot of progress this year and we still have months to go. If anyone had told me how far you'd advance in seven months I would have said it was impossible."

If someone had told Conryu how deep down the magic rabbit hole he was going to be yanked in seven months he'd have said the same thing. Yet here they were. He tried to think how to get his life back on track and failed.

What in the world was going to happen to him? He didn't know the answer to that question and it scared him more than a little.

Chapter 8

In Between

"Woo-hoo!" Sonja shouted as the go cart leapt over a hill and went airborne. When the cart landed Conryu wrestled with the steering wheel, trying to keep them out of the woods. He was doing his best to stay near the edge of the grounds so they didn't tear up the soft earth. The frost had only gone out a week ago and this was the first day they'd deemed it warm enough for a test drive. That combined with the fact that finals started in three days meant it was today or never.

The controls were loose jointed and had at least six inches of play whichever way he turned the wheel. Still, considering they'd slapped it together in about twenty hours, the Blinky Mobile, as Sonja christened it, was handling her maiden voyage pretty well. They hadn't flipped, crashed, or exploded so Conryu was happy.

What they had done was gather an audience. Scores of students and teachers had come outside to watch their mad rush around the grounds. Conryu grinned, for once not caring that everyone was staring at him. They hit the beach, fishtailed a couple times in the sand, and roared on.

"Can it go any faster?" Sonja's blond hair was blowing in the wind and he hadn't seen her this happy since the Brawl.

They'd altered the magic so the engine's speed was controlled by the one who activated it. Conryu wasn't overly confident in his crude transmission, but then he didn't really care if the cart survived beyond today's joyride so he willed it to rev up and the motor obliged.

Sand flew and they shot down the beach like madmen. He slowed a fraction and turned back onto the grounds. The plan was to make a full circle and end up back at the shack. If they survived Crystal said she might go for a ride too.

Sonja braced herself as they went flying over another hill. The second half of the trip was a little smoother than the first as he grew more comfortable with the steering. They finally skidded to a stop beside the shack. The earth magic brakes Crystal had dreamed up worked like a charm.

"That was awesome!" Sonja leapt out of the cart and danced around like a six-year-old.

Conryu couldn't argue. It wasn't his bike, but the cart was a hell of a lot of fun to drive.

"Did you write your parents yet?" He wanted to ask when he had her in a good mood.

"I sent the letter Monday, but I haven't heard back yet. I hope they don't get mad."

Conryu had finally convinced Sonja to tell her parents she wanted to do something besides work at their factory. She'd sent their engine designs to a magical engineering firm and they'd been impressed. Sonja thought they might offer her a job.

Crystal watched them, smiling and shaking her head. Before he could ask her if she wanted to go for a spin Dean Blane landed a few feet away and marched over.

He winced. They'd torn the lawn up a little, but it was nothing ten minutes of earth magic couldn't fix.

"So you got it running." The dean looked the go cart all over. "I have to say, when you told me about the magic engine I had my doubts, but it works."

"Sonja and Crystal deserve all the credit." Conryu leaned back in his crude seat. "I'm just a mechanic."

The dean jumped in beside him. "Take me for a ride."

He glanced at Sonja and Crystal who gave him the thumbs up. "Hang on."

Conryu willed the engine to life and they went roaring down the path. Now that he was getting comfortable he took the turns even faster, one time getting up on two wheels. When they finished Dean Blane's hair was going every which way and she had the biggest grin he'd ever seen.

"I think I may appropriate this for my personal use. Switch places with me, I want to drive."

Conryu hopped out, deactivated the engine, and moved to the passenger seat. When Dean Blane had settled in the tires spun and they shot down the path. Though she didn't set as furious a pace as Conryu, Dean Blane went right along and two minutes later they were back where they started.

Despite the breeze sweat covered her forehead. "That really drains you, doesn't it?"

Conryu hadn't noticed much of a drain and when he said so she smiled and shook her head, muttering about youth.

"Just don't overdo it. You have finals in three days." With that she flew back to the main building.

Conryu spent the next hour giving rides to anyone that wanted one, including Maria and Kelsie. When he finished he collected Prime from the shack and headed to his room, suddenly in need of a nap.

* * *

A revving engine drew Lady Mockingbird to the window. The idiot boy had built a go cart and was racing the thing around the grounds. She'd heard the rumors that the golem club had moved on to making a magic engine and dismissed them as foolish gossip. It appeared it wasn't gossip after all, but the project wasn't any less foolish. Why would anyone bother to create something that only one in ten thousand people could use?

She slid the curtain shut. Let the abomination enjoy himself. By the end of the week he'd be dead and forgotten. It was time to place the final ingredient into the Chimera Jar.

Her three strongest light magic wizards were waiting for her in the casting chamber. After the debacle with the basilisk she'd made a point of having multiple wizards of the proper alignment on hand to control the spirit she summoned.

It galled her to have to rely on her subordinates, but there was no way around the fact that she simply wasn't strong enough on her own, outside of fire, to handle the bindings. It was the nature of magic regardless of what her ego would have preferred.

She descended the stairs and entered her casting chamber. The jar sat in the middle of the chamber, right where it had rested since she acquired it months ago. It glowed red, brown, and blue. All she needed now was the unifying light element. An angel would be far too risky so she'd decided to settle for a golden lion.

The standard four girls were in place to maintain the wards and three more in white robes were waiting to seize control of the lion when it appeared. Everything was as ready as possible.

"Wards!" She raised her hands and the girls began their chant. When the protections were in place Lady Mockingbird glanced at the light wizards and they each nodded once that they were ready. "Here we go."

"Through Heaven's light I call the golden guardian. Appear before me, guardian of Heaven's gates, Divine Summoning!" Lady Mockingbird completed the spell and a disk of light appeared. Through the portal walked a lion as tall as she was and shining with golden light. "Now!"

The light magic wizards chanted as one. "Divine chains hold all things in place, Heaven's Binding!"

White chains shot from small portals and wrapped around the lion's neck and limbs. It roared at near-deafening volume and struggled to break free. Inch by inch the chains pulled the divine spirit closer and closer to the jar.

Her part of the casting was done, but Lady Mockingbird did her best to will the lion closer. Just a few more feet. Her jaw clenched so tight it ached.

The lion's glow intensified and one of the chains shattered. It pulled away from the jar and one of the girls let out a low moan. Her light wizards' faces contorted as they fought to control the spirit. Their hands and knees trembled.

Her girls were too weak. This was why she hated relying on others. For the most part they were useless.

She stepped to the side and raised her hands. Lady Mockingbird would have preferred to avoid damaging the spirit, but if the alternative was failure then she had no choice. "Burn and batter my enemy, Flame Fists!"

She punched both hands toward the lion and a pair of fists made of fire the size of pumpkins lashed out, striking the spirit in the chest and driving it back.

With its balance unsettled the girls managed to drag it just short of the jar.

Just a little more. She punched out again and the fists pounded the lion's chest. It staggered back another step.

With a thought she activated the jar. Black tentacles shot out and wrapped the spirit up before dragging it inside.

The girls collapsed, but she paid them no heed. Lady Mockingbird had eyes only for the jar. The separate colors swirled and became one even as they grew continuously brighter. For a full minute the surface of the jar resembled a whirlpool of paint.

At last the light faded. She rested her finger on the jar and probed the power inside. She'd done it. The chimera was ready to be released at her whim.

"Mistress?" One of the girls that had maintained the barrier knelt beside the unconscious light wizards. "The backlash has knocked them out."

"They served their purpose. Put them to bed. If they're strong they'll recover quickly. If not..." She shrugged. They wouldn't be the first bodies she'd disposed of over the years.

* * *

Clair sat in the corner of the Department's spare casting chamber and tried to calm her raging mind. The room contained only the hard, plastic chair she'd brought with her. Everything else was white and silence. It almost reached the level of sensory deprivation. In theory it should help her push past whatever had blocked her access to her magic. In theory.

She stood up, raised her hands, and focused her will. The moment she did blinding pain crashed through her brain and made the casting chamber spin. Three months and she still couldn't cast. So much for theories. What good was a wizard that couldn't use magic?

Terra tried to assure her that eventually her power would return, but the pity in her fellow wizard's eyes sickened her. She accepted pity from no one, least of all a colleague with weaker magical potential.

"Still no good?" Speak of the devil. Terra stood in the doorway watching.

Clair shook her head. "How long can this last?"

"It's only been three months. Try to be patient." Terra walked over and gave her a pat on the back.

Clair almost punched her. She didn't need sympathy, she needed her magic.

"The chief wants to see us."

"Why include me? I'm useless right now."

"Have you forgotten everything you know about magic?" Terra's voice turned hard. "You're still a member of this office, try and act like it. Orin's at his wit's end. The island's in sight of the city and in a week will be within the area we projected was most likely Mercia's target. If there was ever an all hands on deck moment, this is it."

Clair straightened. "Alright, let's go."

The two women made the short trip upstairs. Inside the chief's office Lin was already waiting. Orin watched them from behind his desk. He looked like he'd lost twenty pounds and gained a bunch of new wrinkles. Clair shook off her self-pity. She wasn't the only one with problems.

"Clair?" He raised an eyebrow.

"No change yet, sir. What's the situation?"

He waved them into the empty chairs and sat behind his desk. "I've asked yet again for reinforcements and been told yet again they have no one to spare. Shizuku's offered to help however she can and I've gotten in touch with a handful of the most powerful local wizards. I was vague on the details, but received promises of aid should the worst happen. I never realized just how few wizards of real power there were in the city."

Terra sighed. "Wizards with high combat potential are rare everywhere. That's what makes them so valuable. Will you bring Conryu in when school ends for the year?"

"He's already in this up to his neck. If there's trouble I'll call him, but until something overt happens, I doubt his abilities will be much help. Hopefully he'll get at least a week to enjoy his summer break."

Clair snorted a laugh. The floating island would be in the contact zone less than a week after he returned home. If nothing changed this was going to be a miserable summer for everyone.

"I've received a shipment of five hundred explosive rounds and ten pistols capable of using them. Not nearly enough, but with the conflict in the north still going strong it was all they could spare. Lin's going to take care of distributing them to a small group of officers with the intention of deploying them in the affected area. I have no idea how much difference they'll make, but every little bit helps." Orin favored them with a desperate look. "Any other ideas? Feel free to speak up."

"What about providing emergency shelters?" Clair asked. "Your building and the Department offices are both warded against magical intrusion. Could we move people in the affected area to safe houses like that?"

"Some, certainly, but if our estimates are correct close to half a million people live in the target zone. There aren't enough secure places in the city to protect everyone and we don't want to start a riot."

"And remember," Terra said. "Once the shadow beasts appear they'll be free to move anywhere in the city after the sun sets."

Though she wouldn't admit it, Clair hadn't even considered the monsters simply spreading out as they pleased. Once the gates opened no one would be safe anywhere in the city.

Chapter 9

Set the Trap

Lady Mockingbird stepped out onto the dock behind the sorority house, the Chimera Jar in her hands. She'd traded her red robes for gray to better blend in to the dark night. Not that she expected to run into anyone out on the island, but better safe than sorry. All three of her light magic girls had woken up with no lasting damage from the ritual. That was a blessing since she had already drawn too much attention to the sorority. Three missing students wouldn't be any help.

Tomorrow was the last day of finals and the abomination would be going to the island to take his test. She called the wind and took to the air. All she had to do was put the jar in a place he'd be sure to approach and set the terms of activation. Once she'd done that, his fate was sealed.

Below her stars sparkled on the lake's surface. It was nice to fly without worrying about the cold or snow. She hated winter. When she received her promotion to Hierarch she planned to ask for a posting somewhere warm, maybe the Republic of Australia.

The flight only took seconds. She started to descend to the central clearing when she spotted movement. Lady Mockingbird halted and hovered silently above. From the edge of the woods a small, dark figure emerged.

What was Angeline Umbra doing out here this late at night? Probably making one last check to be sure everything was safe for her precious protégé. Lady Mockingbird went higher. She'd just wait until the crone finished her rounds then set her trap.

She couldn't help smiling. Wouldn't the old bat be surprised when the Chimera Jar opened and the beast slaughtered her favorite?

Angeline puttered about in the clearing. Lady Mockingbird was too high to make out what she was doing, but whatever it was she wished Angeline would hurry up. She didn't want to fly around all night. Angeline went rigid and started to look up.

She sensed me!

Lady Mockingbird flew as fast as she could in the opposite direction to which the head of dark magic was looking. She dove toward the forest, landed on one of the paths, and canceled every spell she had running.

Shit!

Even without her magic Angeline would sense the Chimera Jar itself. She ran down the path to give herself a little more time. When she found a little niche between a pair of twisted evergreens she stuck the jar in it and raised both hands in front. "Sprits of earth and stone hide this object from all prying eyes, Earth Screen."

The jar sank into the ground. Her spell would block even magical sight from locating it. She dashed off again, angling away from the hidden jar. It would be easier to fly, but if she did that Angeline would be sure to know someone was out here and given the numerous attempts on Conryu's life, she might call off the test tomorrow or move it elsewhere. Neither option would give her the opportunity she needed.

Best to stay on the ground and run and hide like she was a little girl playing hide and seek. It never crossed her mind to confront the withered master of dark magic. Not that she was afraid, certainly that wasn't it. She just didn't want to give away the fact that she was present on the island.

She ducked off the trail and into a thick patch of evergreens. She debated another concealment spell, but decided to take her chances.

Five minutes later the tapping of a walking stick on stone drew her attention. Lady Mockingbird held her breath.

Her hunter was right there, twenty feet away, back on the path. Surely the old wizard wouldn't venture off the smooth trail and risk getting tangled up in the brush and vines.

Seconds felt like minutes and minutes like hours. Her heart hammered in her chest and she wished Angeline away like a child trying to frighten away a monster. At long last the tapping resumed and slowly grew fainter.

Lady Mockingbird blew out the breath she'd been holding and slumped to the ground. She rested for a few seconds then scrambled to her feet. She'd shadow Angeline and be sure she'd gone before retrieving the jar and setting her trap. That was the safest way. There was too much riding on this to take unnecessary chances.

* * *

Angeline shrugged and continued down the path. The magic she'd sensed earlier was gone and she couldn't find anything that might be the source. It was probably just a passing pixie and her paranoia combining to lead her on a wild goose chase.

She never used to be this jumpy, but since Conryu arrived it seemed her life had gotten many times more complicated. Not that she blamed the boy. He hadn't put a toe out of line since he arrived, unlike the members of a certain sorority.

No, just being who he was made him a target and she'd be damned if she let anything happen to him. He was her hope for a proper retirement. When he graduated she planned to offer him the Death Stick and the academy her resignation. She was getting too old for this. It was time to find somewhere warm, and do a little consulting and a lot of lying on a beach.

She walked down the path as fast as her achy legs allowed. She'd left some surprises for Conryu and still had one to go. She smiled as she climbed the path. There was no question he had the raw power to deal with her surprises, the interesting thing was whether he had the smarts to figure the right way to use it.

A twig snapped and she paused. That wasn't a pixie. The little wind spirits couldn't be noisy if they wanted to. She doubted anyone would be pulling a prank on her, none of the students had the nerve to try it. After several seconds of silence she continued on her way.

Ten minutes later she reached a clearing on one of the island's plateaus. She drew a circle and delayed summoning. This would be a fun one for him. And even better for her as it was the last thing she had to do before returning to her bed.

When the circle was complete she listened once more for any movement and found all quiet. She shook her head and called the wind. She was definitely getting too old for this.

* * *

Lady Mockingbird feared Angeline would hear her heart pounding when she snapped that twig, but it appeared she worried for nothing. She watched until the old wizard was out of sight then finally relaxed. That had been far too close.

She retreated back the way she'd come, pausing long enough to collect the jar. Back in the clearing she set the jar a little ways away from the pillar that controlled the shield around the island. She crouched down in front of the jar and placed her hand on it.

The magic awakened at her touch and she set it to activate when the abomination entered the clearing with all three crystal keys. The idea of killing him in the moment of his assumed triumph amused her greatly.

She straightened up, her knees popping in protest. Just one more thing to do. She placed her hand on the pillar and willed the runes controlling it to appear. An alteration here and an extra rune there would assure he couldn't escape and help couldn't arrive in time.

Lady Mockingbird wiped her sweaty brow. She'd done everything she could. Time would tell if it was enough. She flew back to the sorority and a hot bath. Tomorrow promised to be an interesting day.

James E. Wisher

Chapter 10

Finals

They were the last to go, of course. If there was one thing Conryu had gotten used to over the past year it was going last, that and getting ugly looks. The rest of his class had passed their finals yesterday and the day before. Maria was doing her light magic final today as well. Conryu had wished her luck before joining Kelsie on the lakeshore.

Speaking of whom, beside him in the rocking boat Kelsie looked like she wanted to throw up. It wasn't motion sickness, there wasn't enough chop on the lake to say so. In fact it was a beautiful spring day, the sun was warm on his face, the leaves were out, and a light breeze filled the air. They each had packs with a day's worth of supplies.

The dark magic final lasted a maximum of twenty-four hours. In fact the first group had needed most of that time to complete the test, whatever it was. They weren't allowed to talk about it beforehand. They'd receive their instructions when they landed on the beach.

"Are you okay?" Assistant Dean Saint sat at the rear of the boat as she guided them to the island.

"Fine." Kelsie didn't make the lie sound believable. Her ordinarily pale complexion had gone ghost white, the black robes she wore heightening the effect.

"Let me guess," Conryu said. "Your mom called yesterday to offer some unwanted encouragement?"

Kelsie nodded. "She said not to disgrace the family name any more than I already have."

"Charming. Don't worry, we'll knock this out of the park. Your mom will be so proud she won't know what to think."

Kelsie reached across and held his hand. He squeezed back, trying to send reassuring thoughts. They'd gotten pretty comfortable working together over the last three months. Kelsie no longer flinched when they used fusion magic. He'd hoped to introduce her to Cerberus, but hadn't figured out how to go about it yet.

Their boat slid up on the beach and they all piled out. He and Kelsie shrugged their packs on and turned to face Mrs. Saint.

The assistant dean pulled a folded piece of paper out of her robe and handed it to Kelsie. "Here are your instructions. That paper is a map. Three locations are marked, each containing a key hidden within protective magic. Your test is to retrieve the keys and insert them into the column you'll find in the exact center of the island. You have one day to complete the test. For the duration a barrier will be raised over the island to prevent anyone coming or going. When all three keys are in place the barrier will fall and I'll return to pick you up. Questions?"

Sounded simple to Conryu. When Kelsie shook her head Mrs. Saint continued. "Then good luck. The barrier will go up as soon as I clear the beach and your time will begin."

Mrs. Saint hopped back in her boat, backed off the beach, turned, and sped away. A shimmer went through the air as the barrier fell into place. Conryu muttered, "Reveal." The shield looked strong, but nothing he couldn't blast through if it became necessary.

He turned back to Kelsie. "Let's have a look at the map."

She unfolded it and he moved closer. Their landing point was marked with a black star. An X indicated the pillar in the center of the island and the three keys were shown as little red triangles. The nearest key was maybe a quarter mile from their starting point. Shouldn't take long to walk that. According to the map it was hidden in a cave.

"Which one do you want to try first?" Kelsie asked.

Conryu pointed at the cave. "May as well do the closest one first, don't you think?"

"Okay." She folded up the map and tucked it in her pocket.

They set out at a steady march, a pace Conryu could keep up for hours if need be. They soon left the beach behind and entered the thick spruce growing at the edge of the forest. The prickly needles scratched his arms through his robe as he tried to break a trail for Kelsie.

"If I'd known how thick the underbrush was I'd have packed a machete." He spat out a mouthful of needles. "You okay?"

"Fine. I'm not as frail as I look."

He grinned. It was good to see Kelsie showing a bit of spunk. He'd feared talking to her mother might have messed her up like at the midterm.

A hundred yards from the beach the thick evergreens thinned out and gave way to mature trees. He blew out a sigh of relief. If they'd had to walk all the way in that scrub it would have been rough.

Now that they had some space Kelsie moved up beside him. A little further inland the ground rose into hills. That was where they'd find the cave.

"So are we going to bother with the fusion thing or do you just want to dispel the wards yourself?"

"I think we'd better do the fusion thing."

"Why? At this point I realize my power is a meaningless addition to your strength."

He glanced over at her. She wasn't frowning or angry, thank goodness. "Mostly I was thinking that the teachers might be watching in a magic mirror and if I do all the work they might not give you credit for the final."

Her eyes widened. "I hadn't considered that. We'll definitely do the fusion magic. Thanks for not lying and saying you couldn't do it without me."

Conryu stopped and turned to face her full on. "I'm never going to lie to you, not unless I'm ordered to. You're my friend and I respect you too much to do something like that. There may be times when I can't tell you everything that's happening, but that will be because others have cautioned me against it or the information might put you in danger."

She blushed and looked away. "Sorry. I'm not used to the truth unless it's couched in an insult from my family."

"Your family sucks. You should spend a couple weeks in Sentinel with me and Maria this summer, see what a normal family looks like."

"Really? I'd... I'd like that. You know I don't think I've ever visited anyone without my mom and that was just business."

"Sure, we'll have pizza at Giovanni's, I'll take you for a ride on my bike, it'll be awesome." They stopped at the base of the foothills. "We have to be getting close. What's the map say?"

Kelsie dug it out again. "It says there's a lightning-scarred oak near the cave."

Conryu searched the treetops. The half-dead oak stood out like a sore thumb amongst the evergreens. It almost looked like someone had put it there intentionally to mark the key's location. Considering they were at a school for wizards that wasn't beyond the realm of possibility.

The oak was about a hundred yards to their left. He set off again. They hadn't taken more than a handful of steps when Kelsie asked, "You don't think Maria will mind if I come for a visit?"

"Why would she? I've already explained to her, several times, that we're just friends. Besides, she'll be busy working with her mom."

"Do you not have to work?" Kelsie asked between gasps as they climbed up a steep slope.

At the top he spotted a cave and since it was the only one remotely in the vicinity of the oak it had to be their target. It was so dark he couldn't see past the entrance. Kelsie was panting beside him so better to wait a little while before they explored further.

"I'll help Dad in the dojo and putter around my friend's garage, but without a work certificate of some sort my options are pretty limited. I don't have any overwhelming desire to spend my summer vacation working a fryer or waiting tables. I tried that two years ago and it sucked."

"No, that doesn't sound terribly appealing. The hard part now will be getting my mom to let me go."

"Let you? You're an adult, you don't need permission."

"I do if she locks me in the house."

He almost laughed, but from her grim expression he realized she wasn't kidding. What a screwed-up family. At least his mother only locked him up for his own safety. "Why don't you just come straight over from school? You're already packed and she can't lock you up if you don't go home."

"I don't know if I could defy her like that. My mom doesn't take that sort of thing lightly."

"Well, think it over. Whatever you decide I'll back you up. Shall we go collect that first key?"

Kelsie stood up straighter than he'd ever seen her. "Yes we shall."

* * *

As they strode down the hill toward the cave Conryu moved a little ahead of Kelsie. It was instinctive and he did it all the time when he was with Maria. Overprotective she liked to say. Better over than under he always countered. In this case it turned out to be a good decision. Halfway to the opening four fire cats appeared in a swirl of flames.

Conryu chanted Cloak of Darkness, dropped his pack and charged. The cats spread out to surround him.

He took out one with a roundhouse kick. The moment he did a second one sprang at his now unprotected leg.

Conryu leapt over it and pointed his right palm with the fingers crossed at its back. "Break."

He landed, rolled to his feet, and spun. Both hands came up in matched gestures. "Break!"

Two spheres of darkness struck the remaining fire cats, snuffing them out in an instant. No threats remained so he canceled the Cloak of Darkness.

"That was impressive." Kelsie had taken cover behind the massive oak tree. "I didn't expect to encounter any physical threats."

"I suspect Mrs. Umbra left them for me as a bonus test. They didn't even look at you, did they?"

"No, not so much as a glance. You think the summoning spell required them to focus on you?"

"Yeah. You don't know any defensive magic, do you?"

Kelsie shook her head. "Only the basic stuff they've taught us. Most of us don't get special training with the head of dark arts."

"If you want to sit in on one of my classes the only requirement for joining is a minimum of two attempts on your life. I think I'm up to four."

"I'll stick with the standard course of study, thanks. Besides, Mrs. Umbra makes me nervous."

"Why? She's been great with me."

"She reminds me of my grandmother." Kelsie shuddered.

Having met her grandmother Conryu seconded the emotion. Mrs. Umbra, on the other hand, was nothing like the domineering master of the Department of Magic. "I think if you got to know her you'd find she's really nice and I'm not just saying that because she's probably watching us."

Kelsie looked all around like she expected to find Mrs. Umbra hiding behind one of the nearby trees.

"Maybe we should go get the key," Conryu said. "I doubt we'll have any more to worry about at this site. Do you want to handle the light?"

Kelsie chanted and an orb of fire about the size of his fist appeared in the air beside her. He waved her toward the opening. "After you."

"I wouldn't want to be rude. Please, go ahead." She sent the ball of fire in ahead of them.

Conryu shrugged and walked in after it. Kelsie clutched his arm and walked along beside him until it became clear the cave was strictly a single-file proposition.

The cave appeared freshly dug. Some earth magic wizard had probably made it last week when they were working on the preparations for finals. Crystal said she'd done some casting to help the teachers get ready, though she wouldn't give him any details.

He brushed dangling roots out of the way. The tunnel didn't extend very far into the side of the hill and they soon reached a circular chamber. A low pedestal rose out of the ground and in the center sat a crystal key. Wards crackled in his enhanced vision, light and fire magic mingled together.

"I think we can handle this," Conryu said. "How about you?"

Kelsie studied the wards and nodded. "No sweat."

She moved behind him and put her hand on his back. Conryu cast the spell, careful to target only the wards and not the key itself. The protective magic sparked and vanished when his ray of darkness struck it.

Kelsie darted in front of him and snatched the key. "One down, two to go."

They retraced their steps and the moment he cleared the entrance the cave collapsed with a whoosh. Kelsie squeaked and grabbed his arm again.

He patted her hand. "Relax, we're the last team remember? The cave was no doubt designed to be sealed when we finished our test."

She released him and brushed a stray hair out of her eyes. "They might have waited until we were a little further away."

He shrugged. "Where to next?"

She tucked the key away and dug out the map. "Ugh! Looks like the next key is on the northern tip of the island. Three-quarters of a mile if we set a straight course."

Conryu looked over her shoulder. "That's rough country." He pointed at two paths on the map. "If we take this one, then that one, it'll be easier walking."

She frowned and looked from the little marker on the side that said "half a mile to the inch" to the paths. "I'd say that route is more than twice as long, but I agree, thrashing through the shrubs is for the birds."

* * *

Kelsie trudged along behind Conryu. The path made for easier walking, but it was still uphill the whole way and she wasn't the world's greatest athlete, unlike her partner. She thought

173

about how he handled those four fire cats and shook her head. It was like they were nothing to him.

He had very little in common with the other freshmen. She wished she could wield her magic with so much confidence. Though at the moment what she most wished was that she could climb the path without her legs and lungs burning. Maybe she should have taken those exercises the self-defense teacher assigned more seriously.

Five minutes later she couldn't take it anymore. "I need a rest."

Conryu stopped and glanced back at her. He wasn't even breathing hard, damn him. "Sure. I'd say we have another half mile or so. Best to be rested in case Mrs. Umbra left another surprise."

"Do you think she might have?"

He grinned. She loved that expression. "I'd count on it. She wants to see how much I've learned."

"You've done pretty well so far."

Conryu looked around then motioned her to follow. A little ways off the trail was a fallen tree. He sat and patted the rough bark beside him. She settled in and sighed, delighted to get her weight off her feet. After a second she dared to lean against him. He felt safe and solid and warm.

"We've done pretty well so far."

She tilted her head up at him. "What?"

"You said I'd done pretty well, but what you meant was we. You and me are a team after all."

She restrained a laugh that would have sounded humorless and bitter if she'd let it out. It was sweet of him to say so, but they both knew she was more of a burden than a help. That he never treated her like a burden made Kelsie like him more than she should.

Sometimes she pretended he might like her as something more than a friend, then she saw him with Maria and knew she was dreaming. When they were together he looked so happy she wasn't certain what the right word was to describe it. That they argued like an old married couple only added to the impression.

"We are a team, at least for a day, though I don't think I bring much to the partnership."

"You're wrong. You bring something important: trust. When you put your hand on my back I know you won't do anything to put me at risk. That one fact makes you the perfect partner. There's only one other person I trust that much and she can't be near me when I use dark magic."

"Thanks." She stood up. Knowing he trusted her sent a jolt of energy through Kelsie. Whatever it took, she wouldn't let Conryu down. "Shall we move on?"

"Yeah." He led the way back to the path and they resumed their trudge.

Fifteen minutes later the path leveled out onto a plateau. She took the map out again. "It should be right around here somewhere."

They took three more steps away from the path. The stink of sulfur filled the air a moment before a black circle appeared on the ground. Conryu stepped in front of her.

Kelsie peeked around from behind him. In the center of the circle was a two-foot-tall humanoid with a tail and bat wings. She might not be the world's best dark wizard, but she knew an imp when she saw one.

It didn't attack, so clearly the test wasn't combat related. She stepped out from around Conryu and they moved closer.

"What do you think?" he asked.

Kelsie didn't know what to think. Clearly there wasn't a key in the area. "Beats me."

Conryu turned his gaze on the imp. "Do you have the key?"

The little demon stuck its tongue out at him. That wasn't very helpful.

Conryu nodded once. "I believe I know what's required."

He chanted a spell she'd never heard before. Dark power gathered and a shiver ran through her. This spell was of an order of magnitude greater than anything she'd ever experienced.

When he finished he thrust his hand at the imp. Its glowing eyes dimmed and its expression went slack.

"Do you have the key?" Conryu asked again.

"No," the imp answered in a dull monotone.

Kelsie swallowed the sudden lump in her throat. She might not have recognized the spell, but she recognized the effect. He cast Domination. That was an insanely high-level spell, certainly higher level than a first-year student should be able to use. What exactly was he learning in his extra class?

"Do you know where the key is?" Conryu asked.

"Yes."

"Where?"

The imp pointed to a spot further down the way. "Buried under a juniper bush." The instant it fell silent the imp and the dark magic circle both vanished.

"Guess he finished his task." Conryu shrugged and started toward the spot the imp pointed out.

Kelsie shook off her surprise and followed. "Where did you learn that spell?"

"That's a long story and I'm not sure I'm allowed to tell it to you. Suffice it to say there was an emergency with a demon and I had to learn it in a hurry."

She stared. Kelsie didn't know anything about an emergency involving a demon so whatever happened it couldn't have been at school. But if not at school, then where?

Conryu stopped and knelt down beside an evergreen bush about a foot around. He tipped it to the side and yanked out a box that resembled the ones the light magic class used in the midterm only it didn't have a latch or seam.

"No wards, but there's something magic inside."

Kelsie renewed her seeing spell. Sure enough the box was ordinary enough, but something was radiating magic from inside. "How do we open it?"

"I'm not sure we do. I think we're supposed to shatter the box without damaging the key inside."

She moved to stand behind him, but Conryu stopped her. "What?"

"You should cast the spell on your own."

She blinked, not certain she'd heard him correctly. "You think I should shatter the box?"

"Yeah. There are no wards protecting it, it's just a simple pine box. The truth is, I'm not certain I can cast the spell gently enough not to harm the key."

She chewed her lip then nodded. "I can try."

"No. Don't doubt yourself. Remember what I said before the midterm. You have to believe the spell will work." Conryu

177

set the box in front of her and took a step back. "You can do it. I know you can."

Kelsie nodded and knelt in front of the box. If he believed in her then the least Kelsie could do was believe in herself. She took a deep breath and focused. Her hands crossed just above the box. Now or never.

"Shatter!"

There was a sharp snap and fissures ran through the pale wood. Kelsie held her breath and the cracks spread. The surface of the box resembled a spiderweb when the snapping finally stopped, but it was still in one piece.

She hung her head. "I blew it."

A strong arm draped around her shoulders. Conryu knelt beside her and nodded toward the damaged box. When she looked he tapped it with his index finger and it fell into a dozen pieces.

He fished out the crystal key and grinned. "Good job, partner."

"I did it." She breathed out the words so softly she doubted Conryu heard her.

"What?"

His face was only a few inches from hers. Before she could think better of it Kelsie kissed him full on the lips.

* * *

When Kelsie's lips pressed against his Conryu was so surprised he didn't pull away for a second. Once he regained his wits he gently moved her back. "That's the sort of thing that might give Maria the wrong idea about us."

"Sorry, I, uh, sorry." Her gaze darted all around, anywhere but Conryu's face.

He sighed and held out the key. Clearly Maria had been right about Kelsie having a crush on him. Had he been unable or just unwilling to see it? Probably the latter. He'd inherited a tendency to ignore anything he didn't want to deal with from his father and any feelings she might have for him certainly fell into the category of things he didn't want to deal with.

"Where to next?"

Kelsie took the key and dug out the map. She unfolded it and frowned. "Almost all the way across the island. I thought this was supposed to be a magic test not a fitness test."

"If you ever find yourself in combat you may have to use your magic when you're tired. I'd say it's a pretty legitimate test."

"You're only saying that because you're in good shape already."

"Look on the bright side," Conryu said. "We're near the highest point on the island. It's all downhill from here."

"You have a sick sense of humor, you know that?"

"So I've been told." Conryu studied the map. "Looks like we need to pass through the central clearing. It'll be a good chance to take a look at the pillar. Maybe find out if there are any surprises waiting for us there."

"You think Mrs. Umbra left a trap at the pillar as well?"

He shrugged and headed towards the nearest path. "Beats me, but I wouldn't put it past her."

Kelsie fell in beside him and they started down a steep trail. Roots jutted out and the tops of rocks poked clear of the dirt. He hadn't expected smooth walking, but this trail was worse than the one they came up.

Beside him Kelsie's toe caught on a vine and she staggered. Conryu shot his hand out and grabbed her before she fell into a patch of raspberry vines. Unfortunately, in his rush to catch her, his hand ended up right between her breasts. Kelsie's face turned bright red.

Conryu let her go as soon as he got her back on balance. "Sorry."

She shook her head, unable to look at him. "It's fine, thanks."

He held out his hand. "Maybe you better hold on until we reach level ground."

"Okay." She grasped his fingers with surprising strength considering how small her hand was.

He had no idea how long it took to reach the base of the hill, but it felt like hours. Kelsie was wheezing like Mr. McShane after a long day in the bike shop. When he tried to let go of her hand she held on for an extra second.

"What do you think about a lunch break?" he asked.

"Any kind of break is okay with me." She slumped to the ground in a thick patch of old spruce needles just off the trail.

Conryu unslung his pack and joined her. He hadn't grabbed much to eat, mostly junk he snagged from the cafeteria before rushing out to the beach. He settled on a piece of jerky, some chips and a bottle of water. Kelsie was busy peeling an orange.

They ate in awkward silence for a few minutes before Kelsie said, "About that kiss, I really didn't mean anything by it. I was just so excited."

Conryu washed down a mouthful of dried meat with a long swig of water. "Forget about it. Nothing's changed as far as I'm concerned. Though I don't think you should do it again."

"I won't, promise." She peeked at him from behind her hair. "Unless you want me to."

Conryu clenched his jaw. Why did everything have to be so complicated? Regardless of what she said over winter break, he knew Maria would be heartbroken if he took Kelsie up on her offer. He couldn't deny a certain attraction between him and Kelsie. She was a pretty girl, but he didn't love her.

They finished their meal and Conryu helped her to her feet. When she tried to keep holding his hand Conryu gently disengaged. He didn't want to hurt Kelsie's feelings, but he also didn't want to encourage something that couldn't happen. He was seriously starting to regret inviting her for a visit over summer break.

Ten minutes from their picnic site the forest path opened up into a wide clearing. At first glance you'd never know there'd been a stadium or that a giant demon snake had appeared and fought half the faculty five months ago. The earth wizards had done an excellent job smoothing everything over.

In the center of the clearing was a square black pillar devoid of decoration. From this distance he couldn't see the slots for the keys, but that had to be their final objective.

"What's that?" Kelsie was looking a little off to one side.

There was something there, smaller than the pillar. He squinted in the bright sun. It looked like a jar or vase maybe. "I have no idea. Maybe it's Mrs. Umbra's last surprise."

He took a step toward it, but Kelsie grabbed his arm. "Let's find the last key first. It's probably best to do things in the right order."

She had a point, but Conryu was eager for a closer look at the jar. Kelsie gave him another tug the opposite way and he sighed and let her lead him away. He had plenty of time. Another hour more or less wouldn't matter.

* * *

Kelsie and Conryu skirted the clearing before starting down another trail that led to the final key. She didn't know what that weird jar near the pillar was, but it gave her the shivers. Maybe she could get Conryu to warm her up. No, damn it, she couldn't keep thinking that way. All she'd end up with was disappointment.

This path was flat and relatively free of obstacles. She would have liked an excuse to hold Conryu's hand again, but couldn't think of one. Maybe if she faked another stumble, but he'd probably see right through that.

Conryu walked ahead of her, setting a slow but steady pace. She licked her lips and found them still salty from when they kissed. Or more likely the salt came from the sweat that poured down her face as the heat of the day increased.

God, what had she been thinking? He was uncomfortable around her now. It was clear in the way he carried himself. She'd screwed up the only real friendship she'd ever had just because she couldn't keep her hormones under control.

Maybe she hadn't ruined things completely. If they passed the final and she didn't do anything else to make him nervous, maybe she could salvage their friendship.

All she knew without a doubt: she didn't want to face a life without him in it.

"Did the map say anything about the last hiding place?" Conryu had paused a little ways up the trail and was waiting for her to catch up.

She must have slowed while her mind wandered. Kelsie jogged over to him, her aching legs swearing at her with each impact. She refused to be a burden. Somehow she'd keep up, even if it killed her.

Kelsie stopped beside him and pulled the map out. The final location was in a forest clearing and judging by how far they'd come it couldn't be far off. "All it says is, 'Enter the clearing and leave with your prize.'"

"That seems straight forward enough. How much do you want to bet it doesn't end up being that simple?"

"No bet. Nothing about this test has been simple, why would it change now?"

He grinned and a thousand-pound weight lifted off her chest. "I thought I saw the turnoff just ahead. Come on."

Sure enough twenty paces further on a narrow trail branched off the main path. It couldn't have been a hundred yards before they reached the clearing described on the map. It looked like a tornado had touched down and tossed trees around like matchsticks.

Conryu peered around the clearing. He must have renewed his seeing spell without her noticing. Kelsie frowned as she cast her own spell. She hadn't seen him renew it up on the plateau either. Was he just maintaining the same spell all the time? An hour of maintenance would exhaust her. If he'd kept his active since they landed on the island, that was hours ago.

She shook her head. It was another example of just how different he really was. She focused on the task at hand.

The whole clearing radiated magic, a mixture of light and water. That didn't exactly help her narrow down the key's location.

After a minute of staring she threw up her hands. "I can't tell anything with all that background magic, can you?"

"Nope. Looks like water and light."

"That's how I read it. What are you thinking?"

"I'm thinking illusion magic is primarily light and water. Maybe this clearing isn't as cluttered as we think."

She smacked her forehead. Of course it was illusion magic. Kelsie needed to screw her head on straight. How'd she miss such an obvious conclusion?

"That doesn't help us find the key, does it?"

"Sure it does. Now that I know the problem, I know what they want me to do. Mrs. Umbra wants me to dispel the illusion. It's the only spell she hasn't had me cast yet so it makes sense."

Of course it made sense. Why wouldn't the teachers expect him to dispel a giant illusion? Conryu crossed his fingers and wrists and began to chant. He went through the spell three times then hurled a sphere of dark magic the size of her head into the clearing.

An ebony wave washed over everything. When the magic cleared the tumbled trees were gone. The only thing remaining in the clearing was a single stump with the crystal key resting on it.

Kelsie walked over, grabbed the key, and did a pirouette that ended facing Conryu. "I'd say that's that."

"Yup. I think we passed. What about you?"

"Considering we collected the last key in under five hours I think we should get the best grade in our class."

"Let's head back to the pillar so Mrs. Saint can come fetch us."

The walk back seemed to go faster. They went straight to the pillar, though Conryu never took his eyes off the jar. Up close she realized the thing was made up of an amalgam of different metals. Why did it look so familiar and leave her trembling every time she looked at it?

Three vertical slots were cut in the pillar. She pulled the first key and inserted it. A rune lit up above the key.

A deep roar filled the clearing. Kelsie leapt back into Conryu's chest. "What was that?"

"The jar." He nodded toward the now-trembling vessel.

"The jar roared?"

"I sure hope so."

The lid blew off and multicolored energy poured out. The streams of energy gathered, forming first a body then three heads. Each head was made of a different type of energy. Earth was in the center with fire and water on either side. All three heads roared to the heavens.

"Oh my god." Kelsie could hardly believe her eyes. "It's a chimera."

"A what?"

A stream of fire rushing toward them cut off her answer.

Conryu raised his hand. "Break!"

A sphere of dark energy negated the fire blast. The other two heads orientated on them.

Conryu scooped her up and ran for the trees.

* * *

"He really is amazing." Emily stood beside the head of dark magic as they watched Conryu and Kelsie in the magic mirror hanging in her office.

The two students emerged from the woods after collecting the last key and headed for the pillar. They'd managed to clear a finals course far more challenging than any Emily had ever seen for first-year students in under six hours. The fastest an ordinary final had ever been cleared was ten hours and that was over twenty years ago.

"I'm not certain why we even bothered making him take the final." Angeline tapped the Death Stick against her chin. "Even with my extra surprises I could have told you the result."

"It's tradition. We're a school after all. Not having our star student take a final exam would be unfair."

Angeline snorted. "You think Conryu would care? As far as I can tell all he wants is to learn what he needs to keep himself safe. Beyond that I don't think he gives a damn."

Emily sighed. Conryu certainly wasn't the most enthusiastic student to ever pass through her school. That was a shame. If he really dedicated himself he had the potential to do almost anything with magic. She could hardly wait until next year when he started getting seriously into the other elements.

"What's that jar? Another of your surprises?"

Angeline shook her head. "I thought maybe you added it."

"No, I didn't. And if you didn't..."

"Shit!"

In the mirror Kelsie put the first key into the pillar. A few seconds later a three-headed monster appeared out of the jar.

"What is that thing?" Emily asked. The monster had traits of three different elements, including fire and water. Which should have been impossible.

"I don't know, but we need to get them out of there. Use the emergency override to lower the shield."

Emily rushed behind her desk and dug a six-inch rune-marked stone cylinder out of a locked drawer. "Got it. Let's go."

They didn't bother with the door. Emily opened her window and jumped out, chanting wind magic as she fell. The wind caught her and soon she was flying full speed toward the island. Angeline joined her on her own mini tornado a moment later.

They flew over the grounds and toward the lake. From up high she could just make out the towering figure of the monster from the jar. It was smashing around the clearing, breathing fire and raising a cloud of dust.

Occasionally a sphere of dark magic would cancel one of the blasts. That had to be Conryu. He was still alive and knowing him he was protecting Kelsie. She clenched her jaw and willed the wind spirit to fly faster. No student had died in training since she took over as dean, now two of the most famous students to attend the academy were in danger at the same time. How had this happened?

They reached the island and hovered over the central clearing. Every so often a streak of flame or jet of water would splash against the barrier. When she lowered the shield they'd be subjected to the monster's attacks as well.

She glanced at Angeline. The head of the Death Stick crackled with dark magic. What had she expected? Of course Angeline was ready for a fight.

"Hurry, Emily. We don't want to lose those kids."

Emily tapped the runes in a particular sequence until they all lit up. She waited for the barrier to lower, but nothing happened. The runes started flashing and the cylinder vibrated. She threw it away a second before the stone exploded.

"Someone's interfered with the failsafe. I can't lower the barrier. Can you dispel it?"

"No. I helped design the barrier and we made it so no one could interfere with the test. As long as we had the emergency deactivation control I didn't worry about it."

"Can he dispel it?" Emily winced every time the monster smashed another tree flat.

"Probably, but he won't."

Emily couldn't believe what she heard. "Why?"

"Conryu has an overprotective nature. He wouldn't risk that creature running wild and maybe hurting everyone at the school. He'll try and figure out some way to deal with it himself. We need to find out who messed with the barrier and stuck that monster in there."

"I know where to start looking. The Le Fay Sorority."

* * *

Conryu ran through the woods, leaping fallen trees, and generally trying to put as much distance between them and the chimera as possible. Kelsie felt almost weightless in his arms. Nothing like a burst of adrenaline to make you feel strong.

Behind them the monster roared and toppled trees. When they reached one of the many clearings on the island Conryu stopped and set Kelsie down. His lungs were burning and his heart raced.

"Are you okay?" She put a hand on his back as he gasped for air.

"Yeah. Just give me a minute to catch my breath. How did you know what that thing was?"

"My family made it."

"What?"

"The Chimera project was commissioned by the military. They were looking for a weapon they could deliver behind enemy lines and activate remotely. We had a team researching it at Kincade West. They'd managed to fuse multiple elemental spirits and hold them within a jar. What they hadn't figured out was how to control the monster they'd made. Fusing multiple elements into a single creature drove it insane."

"I didn't think you were all that involved with your family business." Conryu had his breathing under control now. He turned back toward the clearing where the mad thing was tearing up the forest.

"I'm not, but Mom couldn't stop talking about it over winter break. The company has a lot of money invested in the project and it looked like she was going to have to pull the plug. The day before I left to return to school someone broke into the lab, stole the prototype, and killed several employees. No one could figure out what happened to it. I guess we know now."

"I guess we do. So how do we kill it?"

Kelsie hugged herself. "I don't know. The team never made one this powerful. They only used minor spirits. When they finished the experiment the wizards blasted it with dark magic until it burst."

"So I just need to hit it with enough dark magic to break the bonds holding it together?"

Her laugh held a hysterical edge. "Yes, that's all you need to do. But I doubt even you could conjure enough dark magic to destroy a chimera that size."

The roars and crashing were getting louder. "We need to put some distance between us and that thing. There's someone I want you to meet. He might be able to help."

They started down a trail at an angle away from the rampaging chimera. Conryu unslung his pack and dug out Prime. Kelsie gasped when Prime flew up on his own.

"Kelsie, this is Prime, my scholomantic. Prime, Kelsie, my dark magic partner."

"Charmed," Prime said. "What sort of mess have you gotten into now, Master?"

"I thought you'd know, given our connection."

"You stuffed me in that sack so I decided to take a nap. The mess?"

Conryu gave Prime the short version of Kelsie's story. "Any idea how we can crush that thing?"

"I assume it's held together with light magic?"

"That's right." Kelsie ducked under a tree branch. "It has a light magic core inside the earth body."

"Then we need to blast a hole through the body then hit the core with Dispel." Prime said it as if this would be the simplest thing in the world.

"I don't know any magic that would blow away that much earth."

"Not yet you don't." Prime opened and flipped through pages.

Conryu stopped and studied the page Prime settled on. "Death Spiral. A dark magic spell designed to smash through magically hardened defenses."

Kelsie moved to stand beside him. "That's a new one to me. Looks complicated."

It certainly did. The chant was twenty words long and needed to be repeated three times. At least the gesture was simple, a twirl of the finger to give the magic the appropriate shape. Under ideal circumstances it would take him days of practice to master the spell. A distant roar indicated he didn't have days.

"Never fear, Master. Since it's an emergency I can feed the words of the spell directly into your mind. All you need to do is repeat after me."

"Alright, but how big a hole will this spell make? The chimera is huge. I could blast through it and never reveal the core."

Prime chuckled. "With your power behind it the spiral will hollow the beast out. The important thing to remember is, you need to hit it chest on. That way you'll bore through the narrow way."

"And you'll have to be quick," Kelsie added. "The chimeras were designed to heal rapidly."

"Okay, but the real question is how will I avoid getting blasted to bits while I'm chanting that crazy-long spell?"

Prime flexed his cover. "That's outside my area of expertise."

* * *

They settled on the simplest plan possible. They'd sneak closer to the chimera and Conryu would cast the spell as quietly as he could in hopes that the monster wouldn't notice. There was a good deal of hoping in their plan, but given their limited knowledge and experience it would have to do.

They left the trail and entered the woods. Moving amongst the trees should make it harder for the chimera to spot them.

"Are you sure you wouldn't rather stay behind?" Conryu asked.

Kelsie was thrashing around through the branches behind him and making enough noise for a small army. "We're partners, right? Where you go, I go."

He figured she'd say that, but he wanted to at least make the offer. This wasn't a simple test anymore and the chimera wasn't one of Mrs. Umbra's extras. It wouldn't ignore Kelsie the way the fire cats did.

Conryu glanced back and met her gaze. There was no doubt or hesitation in her eyes, only determination. Good, anything less would likely get her killed and him along with her.

The monster's roars grew louder and louder the closer they came. It almost sounded in pain.

"Of course it's in pain," Prime said. "Forcing all those different spirits into a single body creates pressure and tension. It's trying to tear itself apart while the light magic tries to hold it together."

"What sort of lunatic would create such a thing?" He looked back at Kelsie. "No offense."

"None taken. I often think my family is more or less all mad. My hope is that it isn't something we grow into."

Conryu grinned. At least she hadn't lost her sense of humor.

They were getting close now. He slowed his pace and eased up between the trees. He crouched down beside a big fallen spruce and peeked around it.

Kelsie came up next to him, their cheeks almost touching. The chimera was in the middle of a new clearing, stomping on the trees it had knocked down. The water head snapped at the fire head which roared back.

The earth head in the center came down between them. The monster was literally at war with itself.

"It's kind of pitiful."

"Yes. Put it out of its misery, Master."

Conryu nodded. Seeing the thing up close, watching it writhe and twist... Destroying it would indeed be a kindness.

He raised his right hand. Prime sent the words into his mind. "Deepest darkness twist and writhe. Grind and smash what I despise. Break through bonds and destroy all barriers, Death Spiral."

He made it through once with no trouble; the chimera was too distracted to notice him. When he began the second pass and real power started to gather around him, the earth head popped up and looked around.

Conryu focused on the spell, but didn't take his eyes off the monster. If it made any move toward them he'd have to abandon the casting and run for it.

Three-quarters of the way through the second chant the fire and water heads popped up. All three heads swung this way and that. They sensed his magic, but couldn't figure out where it was coming from.

He finished the second recitation and began the third. He only made it through three words before all three heads focused on him. Not good.

Kelsie broke cover and ran to the right. The chimera turned its gaze on her.

Sensing his anxiety Prime sent the words faster.

The fire head extended toward Kelsie.

Conryu spoke the last word and twirled his finger.

Flames belched from the chimera an instant before his Death Spiral crashed into its chest. The impact of the spell shoved the chimera aside. The flames struck behind Kelsie, but the force of the blast sent her flying into the brush.

Conryu started to go to her.

"Master, the core."

Conryu turned back. The spiral had bored a tunnel through the chimera's body and revealed a pulsing sphere of light magic. He raised his hand, fingers crossed. "Break!"

Conryu put all of his will into it and a bigger than usual orb of darkness streaked out. Dark magic hit light and snuffed it out. The water head splashed to the ground, the flames fizzled, and several tons of earth and rock collapsed in a heap.

He blew out a breath. "Kelsie!"

Smashing his way through the brush Conryu reached his partner's side. She lay on the ground, limp and unmoving. Her left side was a mass of burns and her calf was pierced by a shaft of broken wood. Only the weak rise and fall of her chest gave any indication she still lived.

They hadn't brought any first aid gear. Conryu tore off his robe and bundled it under her head. What was he supposed to do? He was good at breaking things, not healing.

Maybe he should pull that piece of wood out while she was still unconscious. He grasped the shattered end, pulled the foot-and-a-half-long shaft out and tossed it away. Blood immediately started to ooze out of the hole.

He put his hand over it and pressed hard. The blood "Shit!"

Conryu adjusted her head and tore one of the sleeves off his robe. He wrapped it around her calf several times and tied it tight. The burns were completely beyond him.

"Prime! Do you know any healing magic?"

"I'm sorry, Master. Light magic is anathema to me."

"Damn it!" He took Kelsie's hand. "You can't die. Come on."

He closed his eyes and focused. Magic was all about willpower. If he could control demons with nothing but strength of will, surely he could heal his friend.

Come on, come on.

In his mind Conryu pictured the burns healing and the wound on her calf closing. Warmth flowed out from his hands as pain throbbed in his head.

"Master."

Conryu opened his eyes. Where before there was only charred and blistered flesh now pink heathy skin covered Kelsie's side. He untied his makeshift bandage. Only a small round scar remained where the wood had pierced her.

"How is this possible, Master? You are a dark wizard of immense might. You shouldn't be able to use light magic beyond the most simple spells, and certainly not with force of will alone."

He sat beside Kelsie and held his pounding head in his hands. While he waited for the backlash to subside Conryu told Prime about his Choosing.

"All six gems reacted? Even my creator didn't foresee such a possibility. You are truly a worthy master."

"Thanks. Now stop talking before my head explodes."

Chapter 11

Sorority Battle

Lady Mockingbird lounged on a velvet sofa in her otherwise empty casting chamber and watched the abomination run from her chimera. She was pleased she'd taken the time to leave a wind spirit behind when she placed the jar. This show was far better than anything on television.

The monster that emerged from the jar far exceeded her expectations. It made all the effort she'd expended summoning and binding spirits worthwhile. With a bit of luck she might rid the world of the Kincade brat as well.

The image on her magic mirror flickered as the wind spirit fought her mental command to move closer to the chimera. Lady Mockingbird couldn't really blame the little pixie, she wouldn't have wanted to fly close to the rampaging creature either.

Someone knocked on her casting chamber door. She scowled. Lady Mockingbird had left strict instructions that she didn't wish to be disturbed.

197

The image in the mirror vanished and she stood up. She wrenched the door open and standing there with her gaze lowered was one of her second years. "What?"

"Apologies, Mistress, but Dean Blane and Mrs. Umbra are here. They do not appear to be in good spirits."

Lady Mockingbird growled. If they were here they either knew or strongly suspected she was behind the chimera. She might talk her way out of this—might—but the odds weren't in her favor. "Warn Demarlza and the other more zealous members. It may come to a fight."

The sophomore dared to look up. "Is a fight with the dean and the head of dark magic a good idea, Mistress?"

Lady Mockingbird backhanded the girl hard enough to spin her around. "Of course it's not a good idea, but there are only two of them. We may eliminate an additional pair of the order's enemies. Now go warn the others. If I can deflect them, fine, if not we need to be ready."

"Yes, Mistress." The second year whimpered and ran off.

Stupid child. Did she imagine Lady Mockingbird didn't realize a fight with two of the most powerful wizards in the world, much less at the school, wasn't a prudent move? If the dean discovered what she'd been doing Lady Mockingbird would end up in the Lonely Rock beside the order's leader and all the other wizards guilty of inappropriate use of magic. That was a fate she couldn't accept.

Better to die killing enemies of the order. She only wished she could have witnessed Conryu's death at the fangs of her chimera or better yet killed him herself with her own magic.

* * *

Emily and Angeline stood in the tiled entryway and waited for Amelia to show herself. The First Sister of the sorority would be full of excuses, but this time Emily didn't plan on leaving until she'd checked every nook and cranny of the building. If they'd put so much as a hair out of line she'd ban the whole bunch. Emily couldn't actually kick the students out, but she could fire their poison-tongued mistress and keep them from gathering and plotting. That alone would make this exercise worthwhile.

"Rather gaudy place, isn't it?" Angeline waved the Death Stick in an all-encompassing gesture.

Though Angeline kept her emotions fully in check Emily recognized the subtle crinkling around her eyes along with a little extra hardness in her generally stern expression. The head of dark magic was furious that someone had taken another shot at her prize pupil. Emily pitied anyone that crossed her today.

"I think they decorated the place like a Kingdom cottage. Or at least what they thought one should look like."

Angeline grunted and turned to her left. Emily heard the approaching footsteps a moment later. Amelia swept into the entry hall, her red robe swirling behind her. Something was different about her today. She seemed more confident, almost eager to see them.

Every bit of intuition in Emily screamed that something was wrong, but she couldn't act based on a feeling.

"Emily, Angeline, what a wonderful surprise. What brings you fine ladies to our humble sorority?"

She was mocking them, but in a polite way. Emily wiggled her fingers and drew down her focus. It would come to a fight, she knew it.

"There's been another attack on Conryu. Since your sorority is at the top of my suspect list I intend to search the premises.

"Your theories aren't sufficient cause to poke your noses into our sorority."

"I'm dean of this school and my authority is all I need to examine any building or room on campus. You should know that. It's spelled out clearly in the student manual."

"So it is. Where would you like to start?"

"Your casting chamber," Angeline said in a tone that brooked no argument.

Amelia offered a brittle smile. "Certainly, right this way." Her gaze darted left just for a second.

Emily caught a glimpse of half a dozen older students gathered in the drawing room. They all wore angry, eager expressions. In the middle of the pack was Demarlza, the fire wizard she was certain had led the first attack on Conryu.

They followed Amelia along a short hall to a door that led to stairs down to the basement. This might complicate things—fighting in an enclosed space would let the enemy concentrate their magic. At the bottom of the steps Amelia went to the first door and opened it for them.

"Right through here."

Emily went in first. There wasn't much there, just a sofa and magic mirror. Casting chambers were usually kept empty. Why was there a sofa in here?

"Watching something interesting?" Angeline walked over to the mirror and tapped it with the Death Stick.

An image flickered to life. A black spiral blasted through the chest of the monster exposing a glowing sphere. A moment later an orb of dark magic streaked in and destroyed it. The creature collapsed into so much rubble.

Angeline grinned and tapped the mirror again, breaking the connection. "Impressive, the boy learned Death Spiral. And under adverse conditions as well."

"No!" Amelia shouted. "He was supposed to die."

In the doorway behind her the students from upstairs had gathered.

"I don't suppose you'll come along quietly?" Emily asked.

Amelia thrust a hand forward and hurled a stream of fire. The blue-orange flames struck an impenetrable black barrier.

Angeline held the Death Stick horizontally in front of her, dark magic crackling around the silver skull. "You think you can threaten my student and get away with it?"

She slashed the Death Stick toward the group blocking the doorway. A wave of dark magic blasted Amelia and her followers back and stripped away the defensive magic they'd already cast.

Amelia was the first to her feet. "You think you can best a Sub-Hierarch of the Le Fay Society, hag?"

Angeline snorted a dry laugh and crooked a knobby finger. "This one's mine. Can you handle the pups?"

Emily nodded and eyed the handful of students collecting themselves after the blast of dark magic. There were two seniors, they would be the most challenging. The rest were a mix of third- and second-year students.

Demarlza was the first to her feet. She snarled and summoned a pair of fire cats. She wasn't an especially attractive girl to begin with and the ugly expression she wore did nothing to help.

Emily summoned a pair of wind wraiths. The invisible spirits hung in the air beside her. Since it was six against one she'd have to fight defensively.

Her pulse pounded in her ears and power crackled around her fingers. Emily hadn't been this excited in years.

* * *

Conryu sat in the brush and held his throbbing head. The effects of the magical backlash had let up a little, but damn little. Prime was floating well above them keeping a look out for any approaching threats. After the chimera he had serious doubts that anything nasty remained on the island, but at this point he wasn't prepared to take it for granted. Considering the shape he was in at the moment Conryu doubted he could handle a fire cat, much less a stronger opponent.

Beside him Kelsie groaned. He raised his head in time to watch her trying to sit up. Conryu held out his hand.

She took it and he pulled her to a sitting position. "How are you feeling?"

"Better than I have any right to be. You healed me."

He nodded and winced as the movement brought on another stab of pain. "Yeah. You were in pretty bad shape after that blast."

"I felt your concern. You were really afraid I was going to die."

"If you'd seen how you looked you'd have been afraid too."

"I'm glad I was unconscious. Thank you for saving me. I don't know what I can do to repay you, but whatever you want just ask."

"If you hadn't distracted the chimera when you did I wouldn't have been able to kill it. I'd say we're even. Besides, I don't keep scores with my friends."

She smiled. "How did you heal me?"

"Light magic channeled with willpower." He rubbed his temples. "I don't recommend it."

"Don't worry, I doubt I could channel enough light magic to heal a paper cut."

"If you're up to walking we should lower the barrier for Mrs. Saint. I'll feel better once the school nurse takes a look at you."

"I'm good to go. My leg doesn't even hurt." Kelsie wiggled her foot around as if to prove it.

Conryu climbed to his feet without fainting, then helped Kelsie up. The pain behind his eyes was already receding, thank goodness. He broke a path through the brush and branches back to the nearest trail.

Prime flew down beside them. "There's smoke coming from one of the little houses on the lakeshore."

"The sorority bungalows?" Kelsie said. "Which one?"

"The farthest from the school."

"The Le Fay Sorority." Conryu clenched his jaw. He'd bet his bike they were behind the attack. Someone else must have figured it out as well. "We need to get over there."

He stumbled as a fresh pain stabbed through his brain.

Kelsie slipped his arm around her shoulders. "You're in no condition to go anywhere and I'd only be in the way."

He couldn't argue with that, at least for the moment. The two of them stumbled along like the walking dead until they reached the central clearing. The jar sat in the same place near the pillar, both seemingly undamaged by the monster.

Kelsie went to the pillar while he continued on to the jar. For such a small thing it certainly caused a lot of trouble.

He pointed his hand at it. "Shatter!"

It blew into a dozen pieces. There, no one else would have to worry about fighting a chimera for a while and no spirits would be tortured into such an obscene form.

"Conryu."

He winced. "Did you want to take that back to your mom?"

"I don't care about the jar, we have another problem."

He suppressed a groan. There was always another problem. Conryu joined Kelsie beside the pillar. She held up one of the keys. It had snapped in half.

"Shit! Looks like we're stuck here until morning."

"Do we still pass if we break a key?"

Conryu couldn't have cared less if he passed or failed. Mrs. Umbra had all but admitted the classes and tests didn't really apply in his case. Kelsie, on the other hand, seemed genuinely worried. Given her family situation he wasn't surprised.

"I suspect defeating an unknown magic beast will get us enough extra points to make up for the broken key. How do you want to kill the next eighteen hours?"

"Let's go down to the beach and see what's happening at the sorority."

Conryu shrugged and started out. It wasn't like there was anything else to do.

* * *

Angeline twirled the Death Stick, creating a shield of dark magic that negated the stream of flame roaring out of her opponent's hand. So complete was her defense that she didn't even notice the heat. She hadn't been in a real fight in years. The rush of adrenaline mingled with a burst of fear set her heart racing. Angeline had missed that rush these past years teaching.

Finally the fire ended. Angeline was only distantly aware of roars and explosions coming from other areas of the building.

"Cloak of Darkness!" Angeline covered herself in liquid darkness.

"Shroud of Flame!" Flames swirled around Amelia as she countered with a defensive spell of her own.

"By your name I call you, by my will I bind you. Rise, hell hounds!"

A hell gate opened on either side of Angeline and two dogs as black as a moonless night stalked out. Each of them stood as tall as her, their eyes burning with a red glow. The servants of Cerberus snarled.

"Attack!"

The hell hounds lunged towards Amelia who leapt. A burst of fire from the soles of her feet launched her higher and farther than an ordinary woman could manage.

As she flew over the hellhounds she pointed both hands at them. "Burn to ash!"

A torrent of flame consumed the demon dogs. Amelia landed and turned her flames on Angeline who negated them with another dark shield.

Amelia panted and leaned with her hands on her thighs.

She had skill, but no stamina. Pity.

"Oh sweet death, lend me your strength." The Death Stick pulsed with dark magic. "Dread Scythe."

Her artifact transformed into a black-handled scythe with a silver blade. Black wings grew from Angeline's back and what appeared to be a billowing black cloak covered her from head to foot.

Amelia took a step back. As well she might when faced with an avatar of the reaper. Dread Scythe was Angeline's ultimate trump card.

She kicked the floor, her wings beat the air, and she launched herself at the woman that had caused her favorite student so much grief.

"Flames of Protection!" The hastily chanted spell called a wall of flames into being between Angeline and her target.

She might as well have not bothered. A casual slash cut the spell apart. With her barrier gone a wide-eyed Amelia stared at the descending blade. The shining silver was the last thing she saw before the Dread Scythe cut her in half.

Wisps of dark magic rose from Angeline as she slumped to the floor, her spell ended. For all its power, Dread Scythe took a toll and she wasn't as young as she used to be.

An explosion shook the building. Sounded like Emily was getting serious. She forced herself to her feet and hobbled toward the door. If she didn't fancy getting buried under a heap of gaudy decorations she needed to leave the basement in a hurry.

* * *

Maria settled into her chair. On the table in front of her was a rabbit with a deep gash in its side. Its ribs quivered as its heart raced. All around her the other students had nearly identical animals before them.

Poor little thing. It was a shame they had to hurt the animals intentionally, but as her teacher said, it was no different than a scientist injecting an animal with some disease so they could test the cure.

She stroked the rabbit's head in a vain attempt to calm it down. "Don't worry," she whispered. "I've gotten good at healing. You'll be right as rain in a little while."

She glanced out the window toward the island. Conryu was out there now, with Kelsie, just the two of them. She swallowed a little growl. She trusted him completely, yet part of her worried that despite what he said Conryu secretly had feelings for Kelsie.

Maria gave a little shake of her head and looked away from the window. Whatever was happening out there was beyond her control. Right now she needed to concentrate on her own final. Bugs was counting on her after all.

At the front of the class Mrs. Alustrial tapped her pointed stick against the chalkboard. Since her conversation with Dean Blane, Maria's teacher hadn't given her a moment of trouble, as long as you didn't count the glares when she thought Maria wasn't looking. On the table beside her was an hourglass filled with red sand.

"All right, class," Mrs. Alustrial said. "This is where you put what we've been studying to practical use. You have three hours to construct your healing ward and repair the damage to your test subject. I have every confidence in you all, but should anyone fail I guess we'll be having rabbit for dinner."

When no one laughed her expression went flat. "Three hours. Begin." Mrs. Alustrial flipped the hourglass.

Maria took a breath and centered herself. She'd been studying the spells so much the past months she saw them in her dreams. The rabbit gave a twitch and she put her hand above it. "The light of Heaven is the light of healing. Take that which is injured and make it whole, Healing Ward."

A white glow spread from her palms down over the injured rabbit. When it was fully enclosed tendrils of power snaked down from the dome and entered the rabbit. As she watched the ugly red wound begin to close, the muscles knitted themselves together over the animal's ribs. Its breathing calmed and its pulse slowed.

Maria grimaced as the effects of the spell began to drain her. Though the power came from Heaven it passed through her and was given shape by her magic and will. Maintaining the flow at the correct pace took great mental focus.

The wound was fully closed and the skin was growing over it when the explosion sounded. At least she thought it was an explosion. It sounded distant.

Her ward wavered along with her concentration. She refocused long enough to restore it, then risked a glance out the window. Smoke was rising from the lakeshore. It looked like one of the bungalows had caught on fire.

A second explosion, louder this time, rattled the windows. Some of the other girls muttered, but Mrs. Alustrial slapped her pointer on her table. "No talking."

She looked back to her rabbit. It was sitting up, nose twitching, and seemed free of pain. The skin had grown back. There was a nasty scar on its side, but she was certain it would survive.

Maria released the magic and raised her hand. "My healing's complete. May I go see what's causing all that noise?" She was the first to finish which pleased her greatly.

Mrs. Alustrial stood up and walked over. She examined the rabbit, running her finger over the scar. Her face twisted into an angry scowl, but she nodded. "You pass. Congratulations on making it to your second year."

Her teacher leaned in closer and whispered. "I'm relieved to be done with you. Mark my words, your boyfriend will be the death of you. Go if you wish. I couldn't care less."

Maria got up, grabbed her books, and strode for the door. She wouldn't say anything, wouldn't give Mrs. Alustrial the satisfaction of provoking her, but she was relieved not to have to deal with the woman any further. Her irrational dislike of Conryu was every bit as stupid as the other girls' attitudes. You'd think someone her age would know better.

She closed the door behind her with a little more enthusiasm than necessary and turned down the hall. She'd passed and that was what mattered. Hopefully her second-year teacher would be more reasonable.

At the bottom of the steps a group of girls had gathered. They had packed in four deep in front of the lecture hall doors. "Excuse me." Maria elbowed her way to the front.

Thick smoke billowed up from the lakeshore. She shoved the door, but it was locked.

"The teachers initiated a lockdown."

She glanced to her left and a little down. Conryu's friend Sonja was standing there and staring out with everyone else.

"What does that mean?" she asked.

"It means we're stuck in here and we'll miss out on the excitement." Sonja sounded like the little girl she resembled.

A pair of teachers flew towards the lake. Maria frowned. How had they gotten out? The roof! "Can you cast flying magic?"

"Sure, why?"

"I think I know how we can get out of here and find out what's happening."

Sonja grinned, reminding her for a moment of Conryu. "What are we waiting for?"

They slipped past the still-gathering students and rushed up the stairs. Maria set a brisk pace, but Sonja kept up despite her shorter legs. Once they reached the top floor Maria went to a door in the northern wall and yanked it open. Inside was a ladder up to a hatch that opened to the roof.

"How did you know about this place?" Sonja asked as she climbed up behind Maria.

"My light magic class is on this floor so I've had time to explore. I caught a glimpse of the ladder when one of the teachers opened the door last month. I figured it had to be the roof access."

"Cool!" Sonja ran over to the edge of the roof. "Check that out."

Maria joined her and her eyes widened. A huge wall of fire blazed in front of the Le Fay Sorority. A small crowd had gathered, but they couldn't move past the roaring flames.

Sonja put her arm around Maria's waist. "Ready?"

The question proved to be rhetorical. Sonja chanted a spell and they were airborne before she thought of an answer. Maria yelped, but the short flight was smooth. From their position above the fire she could see girls pouring out of the sorority house.

A few seconds later the roof blew up amidst a torrent of dark energy. Two figures emerged, but she didn't see them well enough to figure out who they were before Sonja lowered them to the ground.

The little fire wizard released her and wiped her brow. "Whew, flying two people is way more work than just transporting myself."

Maria had just time enough to wonder if Sonja was implying she was fat when the wall of fire vanished. Dean Blane and Mrs. Umbra were herding the students into a group. Beyond them the house had collapsed.

"Guess the show's over," Sonja said.

"Yeah." Maria doubted they'd seen even half of what really happened. Part of her wasn't sure she wanted to know what was going on. Deep inside she knew it had something to do with Conryu.

* * *

Emily had complete confidence in Angeline's ability to handle Amelia. As flames burned into her wind barrier on one side and lightning crackled into the other she had a little less confidence in her own situation. Demarlza's fire cats charged in between the flame blasts.

The fire cats bared their fangs and leapt. Her wind wraiths flew in and scattered the flames until only embers remained.

"No!" Demarlza redoubled her flame's intensity.

Emily staggered under an especially intense burst of lightning. If she kept playing with these kids, they might actually beat her. While she didn't want to kill any of her students, this bunch might not give her a choice.

"Father of winds blow away my enemies, Tornado Burst." She threw her hand forward and a mini twister sent all six girls flying out the door and into the hall beyond. One of them hit the wall with enough force that she didn't get back up.

Emily risked a glance at Angeline. The head of dark magic was under assault from a river of flame, though none of it pierced her shield. She shook her head and stalked out of the casting chamber. Angeline could take care of herself. She needed to convince these kids to surrender before someone got killed.

"If you give up now, I promise the court will take your age and inexperience into account during the trial. The longer you fight the worse it will look for you."

"You think we'll surrender to someone that let an abomination into our school?" Demarlza forced herself up. "Better we die as true wizards than accept such a thing."

Emily shook her head to hear one of her pupils spout such utter nonsense. "True wizards keep an open mind when they encounter the unknown, they don't condemn it out of hand. Only an ignorant, closed-minded fool judges a person by nothing but their sex. Girl good, boy bad. That's primitive thinking and unworthy of a student attending this academy."

Two of the younger girls were muttering to each other. Demarlza must have heard them. She gave the nearest a bat to the side of the head. "We will not betray our mistress. Burn!"

A blast of flames was deflected by her wind barrier.

"Go upstairs and gather the others, I'll hold her here," Demarlza ordered.

The other girls hesitated and for a moment Emily dared hope they might come to their senses, but it wasn't to be. Four of them rushed up the stairs, leaving their unconscious companion behind.

"Just you and me." Demarlza offered a cruel smile. "You don't seem so tough now."

Demarlza raised her free hand and a ball of fire appeared. The instant the spell formed Emily pointed. "Jet Gust."

A focused line of wind struck the fireball and detonated it. Demarlza's concentration broke and the torrent of flames vanished. This one was clearly beyond redemption. "Your breath is your life. Cease to breathe and cease to be, Asphyxiation."

Demarlza scratched at her throat as the wind magic stole the air from her lungs. She clawed and gasped and fell to the floor where she kicked around before going still. Emily shook her head again. What a waste. The girl had such potential.

The tap, tap, tap of the Death Stick alerted her to Angeline's approach. She eyed the two bodies in the hall and sighed. "It couldn't be helped."

"No. Amelia?"

"That also couldn't be helped. Not that she was worthy of our help. The other pups?"

"They ran upstairs, I assume to set a trap."

"Perhaps a display of sufficient force will knock some sense into them." Angeline had a wicked gleam in her eye.

"What did you have in mind?"

"I'll blast a path out of here and you fly us through. Once I saw the boy use Death Spiral I got an itch to try it myself. I haven't cast it since I came to teach."

"I suppose that might work. Did you teach the spell to Conryu? Death Spiral seems a bit stronger than what we'd discussed."

"No, I suspect his book taught him. There isn't much regarding dark magic the scholomantic doesn't know. I'm impressed he managed to cast it so well so quickly."

"I agree. Perhaps next year we should design a new course of study for him. I won't bother submitting it to the Department for approval. As long as he passes the midterms and finals they won't care how we go about teaching him."

"That's an excellent idea. Have we given them enough time to get nervous?"

"I think so. Whenever you're ready." Emily moved back to give Angeline some extra room as well as making sure she wouldn't get caught in any magic spillover.

Angeline chanted and spun the Death Stick in a slow circle. Dark magic gathered around the silver skull. When she'd built up the necessary power she thrust the Death Stick at the ceiling. A spiral shot out, smashing through the ceiling and carrying the debris along with it.

Emily moved back beside Angeline. "Father of winds, carry us into your domain. Air Rider."

The wind gathered around them, strong but gentle, and carried them through the floor and up out of what remained of the roof.

A group of sorority members had raised a wall of flames to hold off the approaching students and teachers. Girls poured out of the collapsing house and onto the field outside.

Emily guided them to the ground between the students and the house. The remains of the building collapsed at the same moment they landed. It was an unintentional but powerful bit of symbolism.

The girls faced them, hands raised and ready to cast.

Emily held her hands to the side in a gesture of peace. "Your leaders are dead as is the sorority. Whether you face a wizards' tribunal or we bury you at the bottom of the lake is up to you."

At that moment Assistant Dean Saint rose up behind them on the head of a water serpent. That was the final straw. The rebellious students threw up their hands in surrender and the wall of flames vanished.

Teachers rushed down to join them and Emily directed the new arrivals to take the sorority members into custody.

Now that everything seemed under control Hanna landed beside them. "Looks like I missed the excitement."

"On the contrary, your timing couldn't have been better. Your water serpent knocked the fight out of them and allowed us to avoid any more deaths. I'm grateful beyond words for that."

"How's the boy?" Angeline asked.

"Conryu and Kelsie are fine. They were sitting on the beach watching the fireworks. He lost his robe somewhere on the island, but other than that they didn't have any visible damage."

Emily sighed. "All and all as good a result as we could have hoped for. Did you take them to the nurse's office?"

"No, the barrier is still up."

Angeline frowned. "I know they collected all their keys. What's the hold up?"

Hanna shrugged. "I couldn't get close enough to ask."

Emily patted Angeline on the shoulder. "We'll find out in the morning. Right now we have a mess to clean up."

* * *

The pops and flashes from the sorority bungalow had ended hours ago. The sun hung low in the sky as Conryu dragged the last dry branch into the pile he'd made on the beach. Kelsie lounged on the sand and stared up at the sunset. She'd offered to help him gather wood, but he didn't want to risk her injuring her leg again.

He heaved the stick into the pile and nodded. The pile was almost as tall as he was. The nights were still chilly so a fire would be nice.

Kelsie rummaged through her pack for a drink and walked over to him. "It's a nice pile of wood, but I don't think my lighting spell is going to be enough to get it started." She flicked her finger and a little flame appeared on the tip.

"Getting it going won't be a problem." Conryu moved a safe distance away and raised his hand. "All things burn to ash, Inferno Blast."

A stream of blue-white flames streaked out. After a few seconds he had a roaring bonfire going. Conryu ended the spell and turned to Kelsie. "See, no sweat."

"Where'd you learn that? The only fire spells they taught us in universal magic class was a light globe and how to ignite and snuff out a candle."

"A girl in my club taught me. Maybe you know her, Sonja Chard?"

"I don't know her personally, but my mother regularly curses her family for stealing a portion of our military business. That alone is enough to make me think I'd like her."

"I think you would too, she's spunky. Remind me to introduce you when things calm down."

"She might not be so friendly since our families are in direct competition."

Conryu laughed and lay down on the sand near the fire. "Sonja's about as enchanted with her family's business as you are with yours. It's amazing how much you two have in common."

Kelsie lay down beside him and rested her head on his shoulder. When he didn't say anything she snuggled in closer. It had been a crazy day and he understood if she needed a little reassuring.

When he turned his head to look at her Kelsie was already fast asleep. That struck him as an excellent idea and the moment he closed his eyes he was dead to the world.

The next thing he knew someone was kicking his foot. Maybe if he ignored them whoever it was would go away.

"Wake up, sleepyhead."

Conryu opened one eye. The youthful face of Dean Blane was staring down at him. He started to sit up, but found his movement restricted. He opened the other eye. Kelsie had draped herself over him and his arm was pinned under her, and her leg draped across his thighs.

"I don't want to get up," she grumbled in her sleep and moved closer.

"You didn't bring Maria with you, did you?" The fact that no one was strangling him at the moment argued that she hadn't, but he wanted to make sure.

"Nope, it's just me and Hanna and she's waiting by the boat. You had quite an adventure yesterday."

"Yeah."

Conryu gave Kelsie a shake and she finally opened her eyes. The moment she realized who was there and how she was wrapped around him she scrambled to put some space between them. "Sorry. I was asleep and I didn't realize what I was doing." Her face was bright red.

"Relax." Conryu patted her knee. "Time to go back."

"Almost time to head back." Dean Blane plopped down beside them. "There are a couple matters we need to discuss and there are far fewer ears out here. Tell me what happened."

Conryu did as she asked, with Kelsie chiming in here and there. When he finished Kelsie asked, "Do we still pass even though one of the keys was broken?"

"Absolutely. The fact that you survived that monster would earn you a passing grade in my book." Dean Blane fixed Conryu with a serious look. "You really channeled light magic with nothing but willpower?"

He nodded. "The backlash made the headache I got from dominating those demons feel like a tickle, but Kelsie's okay, so it was worth it."

"I assume you saw the battle at the sorority house?"

"Yeah. Let me guess, they left the chimera for me?"

"Exactly right. Apparently Amelia Light was a Sub-Hierarch in the Society. We'll have to search through the rubble, but I hope to find out more about the group."

"I thought they were a political committee that supported women looking to advance to high positions in the government and at companies," Kelsie said.

Conryu didn't pay much attention to politics, but Dean Blane seemed to know what Kelsie was talking about.

"The Le Fay Society has two groups. The one you're talking about claims to be a nonprofit dedicated to women's issues and unaffiliated with their more aggressive sister organization. The second group is more of a terrorist organization determined to change the world directly with violence and fear."

"Why do they hate me so much?" Conryu asked.

Dean Blane sighed. "The Society believes the world should be ordered in three tiers. Wizards at the top, non-magic-using women below them, and men as slaves and breeding stock at the bottom. The appearance of a male wizard elevates a being they consider little better than an animal to a status equal to theirs. That isn't something they can accept. Hence you need to die."

"Is it me or is that a little harsh?" Conryu grinned, hoping some humor might lighten the suddenly serious mood. It didn't. "Right, so what now?"

"For you two it's a full examination by the nurse. Graduation is in two days. Then you return home for summer vacation."

"I was thinking more about what we were going to do about the crazy people trying to kill me."

Dean Blane clambered to her feet. "I don't know about that, but I think we've rooted out all the snakes here."

Kelsie raised her hand as though asking permission to speak. "But you didn't actually know Ms. Light was a member of the bad Society, did you?"

"Not with certainty, though I had my suspicions. Until she made her move I couldn't prove anything."

No one said it out loud, but Conryu at least was wondering whether there were any other snakes hiding in their midst.

James E. Wisher

Chapter 12

End of The Year

Maria stared in growing horror as Conryu explained what had happened on the island. She'd seen the battle with the Le Fay Sorority, the whole school knew about it at this point, but she'd had no idea what precipitated it. She shouldn't have been surprised it was an attack on Conryu.

"So I destroyed the chimera and healed Kelsie—"

"Wait." Maria was certain she must have misunderstood. "You healed her? How? You're a dark wizard."

She tried to comprehend what he was saying, but her brain refused. If Conryu could heal he really didn't have any use for her. All her hard work this semester had been for nothing.

"Willpower. Anyway, you remember the light gem reacted to me as well. Dark magic is my focus this year, but I have the potential to use all types of magic at a fairly high level, at least Dean Blane seems to think so. You should have seen how excited she was when I told her. You'd have thought I'd given her a million dollars."

They were standing outside the nurse's office waiting while the nurse checked Kelsie out. Conryu had come through with a clean bill of health. In fact, he barely had a scratch on him. It was easy for her to think of him as indestructible, but Maria knew just how near a thing it had been.

"So what happened next?"

Conryu told her the rest including how they ended up on the beach sitting beside a bonfire. Sounded a little too romantic. On the other hand she didn't want him shivering through the night and getting sick either.

"The dean and assistant dean came to fetch us when the barrier went down. Sorry if I made you worry."

Since no one had told her what happened she wasn't as worried as she might have been. "It's not your fault."

"How'd you do on your final?"

"I passed and no one tried to kill me. That's how finals are supposed to work."

He laughed. "Yeah, well, maybe next year. I forgot to tell you. I invited Kelsie to come for a visit this summer. Seemed like it would be nice if she saw what a normal family looked like."

Maria stared at him, her brain not fully processing what he just said. "What?"

"I said I invited Kelsie to come for a visit this summer."

"What?"

"Don't be that way. She's a sweetheart. If you gave her half a chance I bet you two would get along great."

Maria heartily doubted that. She saw the way Kelsie looked at Conryu even if he wasn't willing to acknowledge it. That girl wanted more than to be just friends. "Where's she going to stay?"

"I figured on the couch. The apartment's only got two bedrooms after all."

"She's staying with you?" Maria's voice went up three notches. This had to be a bad dream. She was going to wake up in her bed any second now.

"You don't trust me?"

"With a beautiful girl sleeping twenty feet from your bedroom door?"

"What? You used to sleep over all the time when we were kids."

"Focus on the last part of that sentence. We were kids. You two aren't kids."

The door to the nurse's office and Kelsie emerged. She glanced at Maria and ventured a faint smile. "I couldn't help overhearing. If it's going to be a problem I don't have to visit."

She wanted to tell Kelsie it absolutely was going to be a problem, but Conryu said, "No, no problem. We sorted it all out. Assuming you don't mind sleeping on the couch."

"No, I don't mind. Though I don't think I've ever slept on a couch. It couldn't be any less comfortable than the beach, right?"

"Not at all. I nap on it all the time."

Maria looked from Conryu to Kelsie and back again. They were chatting and smiling like they were perfectly comfortable together. When had all this happened? At least before they'd been a little awkward around each other. Maybe it had something to do with the battle and his healing her. Sometimes using light magic on someone created a powerful bond.

"Are you going to send your mother a note?" Conryu asked.

"Yes, this afternoon. I wouldn't want my driver to come to pick me up and not be there. I'm afraid Mom won't be very happy with me." She grinned in a near-perfect imitation of Conryu. "But that's part of the fun."

Kelsie acted more like his girlfriend than Maria. Standing there with them she felt like a disapproving sister, looking for reasons why they shouldn't do what they were planning.

It sucked.

* * *

Conryu and Maria walked side by side toward the cafeteria. Graduation wasn't an especially big event at the academy. Since only students were allowed on campus they didn't bother with handing out diplomas or making speeches. Instead there was a big group gathering with food and games where the seniors could say goodbye to their fellow students and the teachers.

This year the staff had decided to go all out, with fancy catering arriving by train that morning. Dean Blane said it was to help take everyone's mind off what happened at the sorority. Conryu thought it would take more than appetizers to do that, but he didn't want to sound negative.

The members that surrendered had been taken to Central where they'd face a wizards' tribunal led by Kelsie's grandmother. He shivered, not envying the girls that encounter. He felt bad for anyone that had to deal with that woman, even people that wanted him dead.

"So what's your mom got planned for you this summer? Will you be able to hang out with us a little?"

"I'll just be helping her with whatever I can. I wouldn't want to get in you and Kelsie's way."

He groaned. "Are you still going on about that? What's it going to take to convince you we're just friends?"

"I think you believe you're just friends. If you still believe it at the end of summer break I'll be convinced."

Conryu sighed and pushed the cafeteria doors open. He couldn't figure out why Maria imagined he'd change his mind about Kelsie after her visit, but maybe when he didn't that would convince her. He certainly hoped it did. Things had gotten far too uncomfortable between them.

Inside most of the students and faculty had gathered. As usual Conryu was among the last to arrive. He caught a flash of red out of the corner of his eye and the next thing he knew Sonja leapt at him and wrapped her arms around his neck.

"I did it," she said far too loudly right next to his ear. "They didn't even yell, just like you said they wouldn't. I'm so relieved."

Maria muttered something about him being popular with the ladies before wandering off toward the laden tables to find a snack.

"What's with her?" Sonja asked as he lowered her to the ground.

"Long story. So what were you saying with such enthusiasm?"

"I hadn't heard back from my parents so I called and told them I was taking a job with a magic engineering company. The company was really impressed with what we did on the engine and offered me a good salary. It's so exciting. I may even have a chance to work on golems there."

"Congratulations. What did your parents say?" Conryu guided her toward the food. He'd skipped lunch and was eager to eat.

"They were disappointed, of course, but they said if that was what I really wanted to do it was okay and if it didn't work out I could always come work at the factory later."

"That's about the best you could have hoped for."

Sonja nodded and hugged him again. "I never would have had the guts to tell them if you hadn't encouraged me. Thank you, thank you, thank you."

He gave her a pat on the head. It was good to see Sonja excited.

"Oh, there's Crystal. I haven't told her yet since I wanted to let you know first. Later."

And she rushed off again. Sonja was a lot like a tornado. She appeared and disappeared quickly, but left an impression.

Conryu examined the nearest table and only recognized half the offerings on it. He settled on a deviled egg. The moment he popped it in his mouth Dean Blane approached.

"How would you rate your first year at the academy?"

He swallowed the half-chewed egg. "I lived through it. If the next three are anything like the first, I'll be the first student to graduate with a combat citation."

She laughed. "Next year won't be anywhere near as bad as this one. With the sorority gone and the worst offenders removed you should be safe."

"Emphasis on should."

She shrugged. "There are no guarantees in life. You've come a long ways, I can't wait to see what you accomplish next year."

He spotted Kelsie approaching as Dean Blane left. How was he ever going to get something to eat? She stopped in front of him and hung her head. "Mom found out I was planning to visit you and said I couldn't go."

"And?"

She blinked. "What do you mean?"

"I mean you're an adult, right? It's your decision not hers. What do you want to do?"

She looked away then back. "I want to go with you."

"Then do it. When the train stops in Central tomorrow stay onboard. Show her you have a will of your own."

"Mom'll be furious." Kelsie offered a little smile. "Let's do it."

Chapter 13

Almost Time

Conryu stepped out of his suite and set his bag beside the door, gently so he didn't shake up Prime. After a moment of indignation the scholomantic had agreed to hide amidst his laundry, all clean, thank you very much. He'd come to the conclusion that he'd introduce Prime next year as his familiar since sophomores were allowed to have one, but for now he'd keep it a secret.

Several upperclassmen rushed past him on their way to the train. They still had an hour before departure so Conryu had decided to wait and walk with Kelsie. Maria was supposed to meet them in the lounge upstairs. She still wasn't thrilled that Kelsie would be spending two weeks camped out on his couch, but she wasn't scowling at him all the time at least.

A little ways down the hall Mrs. Lenore's door opened and she stepped out into the hall. Conryu waved. She had on her black robe instead of the pink pajamas.

She smiled and crossed the hall. "Looking forward to your vacation?"

"You know it. What about you, any plans?"

"I'm visiting my family on the west coast. We'll hang out at the beach, surf, fish, all that sort of stuff."

He grinned. The idea of Mrs. Lenore as a surfer chick never crossed his mind. "Sounds fun. I've never been surfing. The beaches in Sentinel City aren't the cleanest. There are a few stretches you shouldn't even walk on without boots."

"That sounds awful. Two blocks from my parents' house is the most beautiful white sand beach you've ever seen. We live in a little town so far off the beaten track hardly any tourists come to visit so we often have it all to ourselves."

"Cool. I have to ask. Why was there a teapot in your bathroom?"

She blushed and looked away. "Students aren't allowed to cook in their rooms so the teachers don't either. Sometimes at night I like a cup of tea and I don't want to go to the cafeteria so I made a little stove with a fire spirit. I keep it in my bathroom so no one will see it."

"That doesn't strike me as a big deal, but rest assured your secret is safe with me." Kelsie emerged from the group room and headed their way. She had on a simple blue dress and black shoes and carried a bag in each hand. "Until next year."

"Have a nice summer."

Conryu left his bag and went to help Kelsie. "Can I carry those for you?"

"No need."

"Are you sure?" If she had as much stuff as Maria those bags had to weigh a ton.

She held one out to him. "See for yourself."

He took the bag and found it weighed next to nothing. "How?"

"Magic. These are Kincade Carryalls. You can put whatever you want in them and they never weigh more than two pounds."

"Now I know what I'm getting Maria for her birthday. How much are they?"

"Ten grand each."

He winced. "Jesus. On second thought I'll just buy her those hair clips she's been hinting around for since April. You ready to go?"

"Yup, all set."

Together they went upstairs. The lounge was almost empty so he had no trouble spotting Maria. After so many days of seeing her in the white robes it almost came as a shock to find her in a black sundress and wearing her favorite silver jewelry. Her bags sat on the floor beside her and she rose as they approached.

Conryu kissed her on the cheek. "You look gorgeous."

"Thanks." She nodded to Kelsie. "Shall we head out? It would be a shame to miss the train."

"You got that right." He hefted her bags in his right hand and groaned. "Are these heavier than when we arrived?"

"They might be. The librarian said I could take a few books home with me. I found three that Mom doesn't have in her collection."

"What are they printed on, slate?" Conryu led the way through the doors and down to the train platform.

Hundreds of girls stood waiting. The babble of voices almost immediately made him long for the quiet of their cabin. The glint of silver caught his eye a moment before the train eased up to the platform.

He glanced back at the school. He wouldn't miss the place, but on the other hand his first year of school hadn't been quite as bad as he'd feared. Close, but meeting Sonja and Kelsie had helped balance out the repeated murder attempts.

He found he was curious to discover what next year would bring.

* * *

Lady Raven stood in the light of one of the two windows in her redoubt and watched the floating island drift ever closer. The edge of the shadow was touching the city now. In a couple more days it would be in place and the Le Fay Society would put the Alliance on its knees begging them to spare Sentinel City.

Maybe they would. If the world's leaders met the Society's demands the island could continue on its way and no one would be worse off for the little scare they'd receive. And if the leaders gave in this time, when next year rolled around the Society would make new demands. It would continue on until the artifacts were found or the trick stopped working.

She smiled. A large piece of Lady Raven hoped the powers that be refused to yield to their demands. How many lives could her shadow beasts take before they were destroyed? It would be exciting to find out. Either way she would have completed her mission. The Hierarchs would have to recognize her efforts and promote her. It was a win-win situation and those were her favorites.

She stretched, enjoying the warmth. Not much longer now.

Lady Raven could hardly wait.

The Chimera Jar

Author Notes

Nothing like fighting a giant three-headed monster to ruin your day. And if you think that was bad, just wait until the next book. Things show no sign of improving for our unlucky hero. I hope you enjoyed The Chimera Jar and will stick with me for The Raven's Shadow.

As always, thanks for reading.

James

James E. Wisher

About the Author

James E. Wisher is a writer of science fiction and Fantasy novels. He's been writing since high school and reading everything he could get his hands on for as long as he can remember. This is his twelfth novel.

Printed in Poland
by Amazon Fulfillment
Poland Sp. z o.o., Wrocław